Praise for
The Wilde [illegible] Gray

"A debauched [illegible] [illegible]ugh time and decadence! Szereto brings an authentically 'classic' voice to this modern tale of Dorian Gray, who descends from masterminding orgies, to slavishly sodomitical obsequiousness, to ultimately staging cruel seductions using his ageless beauty—deeds that can only serve to make his well-hidden portrait grow more monstrous. A sequel that would make Oscar Wilde turn bright red!"

—John Everson, author of *Siren* and *NightWhere*

"Mitzi Szereto never ceases to amaze with her originality and daring. Her imagination seems limitless. In this intensely sensual novel, a hedonistic Dorian Gray is conjured up as never before. With extraordinarily lyrical prose, she paints a portrait of Dorian that will stay with you forever."

—Janice Eidus,
author of *The War of the Rosens*
and *The Last Jewish Virgin*

"Mitzi Szereto writes this compelling story with poetic fluency. *The Wilde Passions of Dorian Gray* is a hedonistic rush that doesn't shy away from the darker side of passion. I loved it!"

—Sam Stone, author of the *Vampire Gene* series

"Adventurous sex, Paris, New Orleans, and countless exotic locations, plus a dash of the supernatural—how could I not love Mitzi Szereto's new novel about the very-much-live afterlife of Oscar Wilde's wonderfully dissolute character? It touches all my buttons and begs to be read after dark..."

—Maxim Jakubowski,
author and editor of *The Mammoth Book of Best New Erotica* series

"Szereto's elegantly written novel picks up where Oscar Wilde left off with the continued adventures of the corrupt and seductive Dorian Gray, a man blessed (or cursed?) with eternal youth and a portrait that ages in his stead. Gray's hedonistic adventures take him from Paris to Marrakesh and beyond as he explores increasingly extreme and inventive debaucheries. Sizzling erotica that would make Oscar Wilde blush!"

—Lucy Taylor,
author of *The Safety of Unknown Cities* and winner of the Bram Stoker Award for best first novel

THE WILDE PASSIONS OF DORIAN GRAY

A NOVEL

THE WILDE PASSIONS OF DORIAN GRAY

A NOVEL

BY

MITZI SZERETO

CLEIS PRESS

Published in the United States by Cleis Press, Inc.,
2246 Sixth Street, Berkeley, California 94710.

Printed in the United States.
Cover design: Scott Idleman/Blink
Cover photograph: William Morris/Getty Images & iStockphoto
Text design: Frank Wiedemann

First Edition.
10 9 8 7 6 5 4 3 2 1

Trade paper ISBN: 978-1-57344-965-6
E-book ISBN: 978-1-57344-984-7

For what shall it profit a man, if he shall gain the whole world, and lose his own soul?

—MARK 8:36

Every saint has a past, and every sinner has a future.

—OSCAR WILDE

The soul is a terrible reality. It can be bought, and sold, and bartered away. It can be poisoned, or made perfect.

—DORIAN GRAY

A NOTE FROM THE AUTHOR

My very first introduction to Oscar Wilde and *The Picture of Dorian Gray* came at an early age. My film-buff father, who'd been a fan of the 1945 film version of the novel starring George Sanders and Hurd Hatfield, bought me a paperback of the book when I was ten years old. Though perhaps a bit young to be reading such a novel, I was a precocious child with a mental age in excess of my years; therefore novels intended for adults were my reading material of choice.

I remember being enchanted by Wilde's beautiful use of language and vivid imagery, not to mention his keen wit—particularly when it came to his observations of society. And like the characters in the book, it was impossible for me *not* to be captivated by Dorian Gray, even when he was in the midst of committing some dreadful atrocity. Although Dorian was a villain, he was also a victim—in this case a victim of his own beauty. When confronted by the inevitability of its decay, he unwittingly acts in a manner that brings to mind Faust, who offered his soul to Mephistopheles in return for knowledge and worldly pleasures. Indeed, literature is filled with Faustian themes—and Wilde's novel is without doubt one of the finest examples.

Yet there's far more to be found in the story than a man's quest to remain eternally young and beautiful. Oscar Wilde was a homosexual man living in an era and country that made such things illegal (he would, in fact, serve a prison sentence for his "sins"). Not surprisingly, there are homoerotic overtones present in Wilde's tale on which, even at the tender age of my initial reading of the work, I did not fail to pick up. Now, teaching erotic writing workshops many years later, I often make reference to *The Picture of Dorian Gray* as an example of erotic literature, albeit in a more subtle form. That Wilde had not planned to be as subtle goes without saying. When the novel first appeared in magazine form, portions were censored by the editors, who deemed the work too shocking and immoral. There was even an outcry from critics that the author should be prosecuted on moral grounds. Wilde ended up performing substantial revisions, not to mention deletions, before *The Picture of Dorian Gray* was finally published as a novel in 1891.

In writing *The Wilde Passions of Dorian Gray*, it has not been my intention to "re-imagine" the original work or revise it by filling in the blanks, but rather to continue from where the tale left off, bringing Dorian Gray out of Victorian London and into the present day, with several stops along the way. Obviously, I have had to take some liberties with the original text, altering the incident of Dorian's purported death in order to allow readers to follow him through time. What I did *not* alter was the nature of Dorian Gray's character. Wilde portrayed him as a sexual profligate and, yes, even a murderer. For Dorian to live on, he needed to become progressively more debauched from when we last saw him, descending into an abyss of degeneracy that perhaps Mr. Wilde himself would never have envisioned.

Be warned: *The Wilde Passions of Dorian Gray* is *not* for the faint of heart. The novel chronicles the life of a man who, in his insatiable hunger for sensation, wallows in sin, corruption, and destruction. When confronted by purity, his only desire is to sully it. You will find lust, perversion, blasphemy, and murder on these pages. But you will also find redemption—demonstrating that evil does not always triumph, and those who perpetrate it can sometimes find a reason to change.

To be here in the twenty-first century, taking this classic nineteenth-century work of literature and creating a new life for it, is something I would never have imagined back in the days of my childhood. I hope that Oscar Wilde, wherever he may be, will look upon *The Wilde Passions of Dorian Gray* as an homage both to himself and to one of the most captivating characters ever to emerge from English literature. As for the sexual content present in the story, something tells me that dear Oscar will forgive me for my indiscretions!

Mitzi Szereto

PROLOGUE

The only way to get rid of a temptation is to yield to it. Resist it, and your soul grows sick with longing for the things it has forbidden to itself, with desire for what its monstrous laws have made monstrous and unlawful.

—Lord Henry Wotton

Dorian Gray awakens as if from the grave. A great weight presses down on him from above, but when he looks up to determine the cause, he realizes it's his head, which feels so heavy upon the stem of his neck that he expects it to tumble off and land on the crumpled bedding beneath him. Even the air itself is heavy, as if he were trying to breathe through cotton wool.

He blinks several times to clear his vision, the effort of moving his eyelids far too strenuous an endeavor to undertake without discomfort; they feel as if cast-iron window weights have been attached to them. The bluish haze that blurs the objects in the lavishly appointed bedroom make him wonder if he has somehow developed shortsightedness. His puffy, burning eyes struggle to focus and make sense of his surroundings. He hears the sound of breaths being drawn in and then released in a steady rhythm that might have been soothing if not for his disorientation. Are they his or someone else's?

Red velvet draperies cover the tall windows and move sluggishly in the breeze as if they too are affected by the overwhelming sense of heaviness that afflicts him. They remind Dorian of curtains in a theater; he expects them to swing open, revealing players on a stage. Instead they reveal irregular chinks of yellow light that insinuate themselves inside the room, informing him that it's morning.

The clarity of his vision slowly returns, bringing with it more detail. Embroidered silk cushions lie scattered across the wooden floorboards, as do overturned glasses and random bits of gray ash. The bed upon which he finds himself appears to be a tangled heap of arms and legs, the more slender among them female. They crisscross in a haphazard pattern. Arms as white as the first winter snow. Arms as black as polished ebony. Some look as if they belong to the same body, though Dorian knows this to be physically impossible. Lying amidst the jumble he detects the gentle curve of a woman's breast and, unless he's mistaken, the graceless wedge of a man's foot.

That Dorian is inside a bedchamber becomes obvious

to him. It might be his, though he can't be certain. He seems to recollect a small man with a pencil-thin moustache and a worn yellow tape around his neck measuring the window frames with extravagant meticulousness, then producing several swatches of fabric, one of which was red velvet. The memory's returning to him in more clarity now. Monsieur Larouche, the curtain maker. His men finished hanging the red velvet draperies a few weeks ago.

As for the hours that have just gone past, they remain a confused jumble of images in Dorian's mind, though the fragrant after-scents of smoked opium and female pleasure tease at the edges of his memory like a tickling finger, gradually bringing him back to consciousness. Painted scarlet lips pulling on the tip of an opium pipe, then later on the tip of his manhood. Secretive openings being filled by inquisitive fingers, as well as other objects not generally suited for the purpose. Yes, the mislaid hours of the night are finally being located!

At some point Dorian must have lost count of the number of times he spent himself, though he suspects it transpired at least once with each person present in the room and likewise with those who have already departed to seek out the familiarity of their own beds. He squeezes his eyes shut and reopens them, the burning less troublesome now. Despite the tiny veins of red marring the sclera, their blue is as pure as the sky on a perfect spring day. Yet the tableau laid out before him is anything *but* pure.

Is that a young man lying unconscious on a heap of silk cushions by the window, or a young woman with short-cropped hair? He'll never grow accustomed to these young ladies who shear off their pretty locks in this masculine manner. He prefers men to look like men and women to look like women; at least then one can always tell who the players are. The figure on the cushions moves ever so perceptibly, yet it is enough. It offers Dorian a pleasing vista of two well-formed hind cheeks that remind him of hot-cross buns. The sight of them makes him hungry, though it isn't a meal he hungers for. On the contrary, his is a hunger that never ceases—and it cannot be appeased with anything so mundane as food.

He blinks again to clear away the last of the fog from his eyes to better enjoy the visual feast draped across the cushions. The figure now moves in earnest, curling into a fetal ball, at which point Dorian's breath catches in his throat. Although the shifting of position has not provided absolute confirmation of the sleeper's gender, what it *has* done is provide confirmation of the activities in which the sleeper has been engaged. The opening brought into view gives every indication of its frequent usage over the last few hours—very likely by Dorian. Perhaps the slumbering figure is male after all. Then again, perhaps not. The ladies of Dorian's society have rarely denied him anything. Nor, for that matter, have the gentlemen.

A soft groan reaches his ears, followed by a rustling as a face appears from beneath the tangle of the duvet; Dorian recognizes Elsa, a dancer from the Folies Bergère. She stretches her well-toned limbs and smiles at him languidly, her pretty features a fusion of sleep and smeared rouge. The brown tips of her breasts point up at him and he lowers his head, drawing one into his mouth. It tastes sweet to his tongue, as if it has been dipped in honey. Suddenly Dorian experiences another flash of memory—that of the famed dusky-skinned *chanteuse* who spent most of the previous evening applying the contents of a jar of honey onto the clefts of the ladies, only to afterward lick it away. He tries to recall her name. Perhaps it will come to him later.

The recollection inspires a renewal of activity in Dorian's loins and he once again reaches full prominence. It is a rare occasion for him to be dormant—one of the many benefits of his youth and his voracious physical appetites, neither of which show any signs of fading. Taking note of his condition, Elsa shucks off the duvet and climbs atop him, guiding his erect flesh inside her until she's filled. Dorian observes the rapid jiggling of her breasts as she rides him and opts not to take them into his hands, but rather to lie back and amuse himself with the performance. Inside the wet warmth of her there is familiarity as well as pleasure; he has been here before. Despite his indulgence in the poppy, there's no slowing down of his response. His release arrives swiftly and in a fluid arc onto his belly as Elsa abruptly shifts her nimble body off of him, not wanting to be got with child. Her eyes twinkle with mischief as she dips a fingertip into the pool of liquid and glosses her lips with it, returning to Dorian more memories of the previous night.

Yet there are some memories he prefers not to recall. Memories of the past that reside in his soul like evil specters, eating away at his flesh from the inside…

Dorian remembers Basil Hallward, the artist in London who painted his portrait, capturing every element of his youth and beauty on canvas—a canvas Dorian can never allow the world to see. He remembers stabbing the artist to death after he insisted on exhibiting the painting, the hideous creature captured within the confines of the ornate frame depicting the sitter's every sin and debauchery. He remembers the attack on his life by the vengeful James Vane, the brother of the young actress he rejected—the foolish Sibyl Vane, who allowed love to lead her by the nose and, eventually, to suicide.

But most of all he remembers his attempt to destroy his portrait. As he raised the knife—indeed, the very same knife that had murdered Basil Hallward—to annihilate the grotesque image on the canvas and thereby eliminate the last remaining evidence of his crimes, a pain of unbearable proportions had coursed through his body, bringing him face-to-face with Death. Dorian had known then that he could neither destroy it nor himself. He had chastised himself for his folly for having entertained the notion that he could, through acts of redemption and repentance, return to his "rose-white boyhood," as his friend Lord Henry Wotton had referred to it, and cause the cursed portrait to return to its original pristine state. His desire for life, his lust for vice, were by then too strongly implanted in him. Lord Henry had done an excellent job on his young protégé. Though surely even dear hedonistic Harry could never have conceived of the monster Dorian would eventually become.

Therefore Dorian had staged his own demise. The promise of a hearty meal and a bottle of wine were more than sufficient to lure an old vagrant to his home in Grosvenor Square, where Dorian led the ragged fellow upstairs to the old schoolroom that was always kept locked and that now contained a duplicate portrait—one from the many studies Basil Hallward had done before completing what would eventually become his masterpiece. Here Dorian stabbed his victim through the heart, then fit the rings from his fingers onto those of the vagrant's. He next set fire to the replacement canvas—a fire that destroyed both it and enough of the lifeless man so that the rings he now wore would be the sole indication as to the corpse's identity.

Dorian Gray was, for all intents and purposes, *dead.*

As for the original portrait, it had been secured safely below ground inside a concrete bunker located in the countryside many miles away from London. It was unlikely anyone should venture near it but a few cows.

By the time news of Dorian's death had begun to circulate through London society, he'd already reached Paris, where he planned to start a new life...

A life which had led him to this bed, with its jumble of limbs and the potent perfume of sex.

LONDON,
189—

The pulse of joy that beats in us at twenty becomes sluggish. Our limbs fail, our senses rot. We degenerate into hideous puppets, haunted by the memory of the passions of which we were too much afraid, and the exquisite temptations that we did not dare to yield to. Youth! Youth! There is absolutely nothing in the world but youth!

—Lord Henry Wotton

The divine scent of roses and opium-tainted cigarettes filled his nostrils. It inspired a curious sensation of longing to swell in his heart, as if what life had given him to date had been found wanting. The cheerful music of birdsong tickled his ears, so innocent in its joy as to be tragic. Did these creatures realize that their fate lay at the mercy of a prowling feline or some other garden predator? Perhaps not, for then their singing would not be nearly so sweet.

Lord Henry Wotton reclined like a pasha on the silk divan, watching his every movement, his every gesture, as if absorbing the life from them. Basil Hallward, the artist in whose studio they sat, appeared very out of sorts despite having just completed a work of great mastery—indeed, one of his best works, if not *the* best. It was a portrait of Dorian Gray, a young man of extraordinary beauty who was poised at the beginning of his life.

The canvas had been placed on a wooden display easel in the center of the room so that those present could admire it. As Dorian studied the painting, he found himself becoming captivated by his own image. He felt drawn toward it like a lover. The arresting blue of his eyes shone out from the canvas, as alive and vibrant as the eyes looking out from his face. The light that had come through the window during his sittings had caught in his hair, turning some of the tendrils into spun gold. It was as if the sun had chosen to shine upon him, desiring to enhance the exquisiteness of the subject still further. The elegantly curved lips matched Dorian's flesh-and-blood versions down to their dewy rose-petal moistness, inspiring an observer to kiss them. At that moment he nearly strode up to the canvas, so intense was the yearning to press his lips to the painted ones that were a mirror image of his own. How very exquisite he was!

Dorian felt a stirring in his trousers as he continued to study the painting. Had it not been his painted self he was admiring, he might have been in danger of owning desires that were not considered proper in polite society—desires that could get one not only condemned as a menace to society, but imprisoned. He found himself curious whether the other two gentlemen in the room were experiencing a similar reaction. Shifting his gaze toward Lord Henry, he was given his answer. Lechery tainted Lord Henry's handsome features and his hand, which had previously lain dormant in his lap, now appeared to be engaged with the rather discernible protrusion straining against the front of his trousers, rubbing it with his palm as if to soothe it. Dorian felt his own similar malady leaping in recognition at a shared experience. With a heightened color in his cheeks, he turned back to the portrait, confused and embarrassed by his feelings and even more so by Lord Henry's reaction. Perhaps it had been a trick of the light caught in the folds of the fabric, for when he looked toward the gentleman again, all appeared normal, with Lord Henry's hand resting in his lap once more. Surely he had imagined the entire episode.

"Astonishing!" Lord Henry cried, clapping his hands together in excitement. "Utterly astonishing! Basil, old chap, you have clearly excelled yourself. This is truly your finest work!"

Basil Hallward remained silent, staring at the painting with an expression of doom. Dorian wondered why the artist seemed not to comprehend the magnificence of his work, to say nothing of the magnitude of his talent for having so successfully captured with paint what was inside the room with them in life. Had Dorian been looking into a mirror, the image could not have been more accurate. There was a quality in the subject's face that made one trust him at once. All the candor of youth was present, as well as all its passionate purity. How could Hallward be dissatisfied with such a fine representation?

And yet he was.

Since their first meeting in the artist's studio, Lord Henry had often been heard to remark that Dorian Gray was a young Adonis who looked as if he'd been made of ivory and rose leaves. Such high and mellifluous praise had at first been an embarrassment, but Dorian came to accept it and even find himself agreeing with it. What he could *not* understand was Hallward's despondency over his creation. His attitude toward it did not alter with time. On the contrary, he regarded the painting with a kind of fatality, as if no good could ever come of its existence. It became a matter of contention between Lord Henry and the artist until, for the sake of preserving their friendship, the subject was avoided.

Perhaps Dorian should have turned a deaf ear to all those philosophical discussions about the fleeting nature of youth and beauty—discussions Lord Henry Wotton always led with great enthusiasm. But he had not. Instead he'd allowed himself to be swept up in them, absorbing Lord Henry's opinions until they became his own. Had it been fate that brought Dorian together with Basil Hallward at one of Lady Brandon's soirees? Both men had remarked often that it was. If so, fate had also played a role in Dorian's chance meeting with Lord Henry on the day the gentleman had chosen to call on the artist at his home. Hallward had seemed almost fearful when introducing Lord Henry to Dorian—even more so when Dorian insisted that Lord Henry remain while he sat for his portrait, which was reaching completion, as was Dorian's tolerance for the boredom of remaining still for long stretches of time.

Such fears on Hallward's part were well founded; Dorian had been left deeply disturbed, yet also deeply moved, by Lord Henry's prophetic commentaries. They struck a harsh chord inside him, awakening a discontent he'd never known was there—a discontent that told him life had more fire in it than most people dared to experience. Dorian found himself mesmerized by every word dropping like a bitter pearl from Lord Henry's lips, intuitively understanding the terrifying meaning behind them. "When your youth goes, your beauty will go with it, and then you will suddenly discover that there are no triumphs left for you, or have to content yourself with those mean triumphs that the memory of your past will make more bitter than defeats," Lord Henry had said. "Every month as it wanes brings you nearer to something dreadful."

The declaration sounded a death knell in Dorian's ears, yet he felt as if he were entering into a trance as he listened. There was something incredibly seductive in the way Lord Henry's voice washed over him, bathing his body in the fragrant oil of its discontent. Despite the unpleasant subject matter, Dorian found himself growing hard inside his trousers.

"Realize your youth while you have it," Lord Henry continued. "Don't squander the gold of your days listening to the tedious, trying to improve the hopeless failure, or giving away your life to the ignorant, the common, and the vulgar, which are the aims, the false ideals, of our age. Live! Live the wonderful life that is in you! Let nothing be lost upon you. Be always searching for new sensations. Be afraid of nothing."

It felt as if everything he said was designed to make Dorian fight to save his life—to save his youth and his beauty and, with them, the desire in his belly for pleasures as yet untasted, unimagined. Every proclamation and prediction from Lord Henry's mouth was a tongue laving his manhood, teasing from it tears of longing. When Dorian looked down at his lap, he expected to see his trouser flap unbuttoned and his erection exposed as a pink flash of tongue took up the moisture that spilled from it. He felt his cheeks burn with shame and nearly cried out, for such wicked fancies had never before entered his mind. Indeed, Lord Henry was saying nothing that should inspire such depraved thoughts, yet here they were, along with those of a more unwholesome nature he dared not dwell upon for fear they could be read on his face.

Suddenly the unspoiled blue of Dorian's eyes clouded over with tears. "How sad it is!" he cried. "I shall grow old and horrid and dreadful, but this picture will remain always young. It will never be older than this particular day of June. If it were only the other way! If only it was *I* who remained always young and the picture that were to grow old! For this I would give everything! Yes, there is nothing in the whole world I would not give!"

How innocent he had been when he'd uttered those words in Basil Hallward's studio—innocent and filled with the folly and vanity that are the domain of the young. How could he have known that a comment made by chance, a mere fancy, really, would alter the course of his life, leading him down pathways most men would never dare to tread?

PARIS,
192—

Time is jealous of you, and wars against your lilies and your roses.

—Lord Henry Wotton

The red velvet draperies continued to move sluggishly in the morning breeze, bringing into the room the smell of freshly baked bread from the nearby *boulangerie* while flushing out the smells of the previous night's excesses. What it failed to do was flush out the memories haunting the young man lying amidst a heap of naked limbs until he was forced to confront them.

Memories. The stuff of the foolish and sentimental. Dorian Gray was neither. The only thing he had to be sentimental about was the vacancy left by his absent friend Lord Henry Wotton—his dear Harry—on whom he reflected with fondness, wishing he could share with him his experiences over a bottle of wine and a sumptuous meal. Lord Henry had always spoken with the reverence of the religiously devout about living for the senses. How proud he would be of his protégé if he could see Dorian now! Dorian considered writing to Lord Henry at his address in Curzon Street, but whether he was still alive Dorian had no way of knowing—and there was no one from whom he could safely inquire. Perhaps there were some things best left in the past—including cherished friends for whom Dorian's adventures would have provided a wealth of entertainment.

Yet there was one adventure it would not have been prudent to share, such as the methods Dorian had employed to orchestrate his own purported death. It was unlikely he should ever learn if Harry's philosophy of hedonism and of life lived entirely for the senses extended to utilizing any methods possible to prolong it, even if those methods included murder. Indeed, it would be the first of many; Dorian's hands had been stained with blood long before the night of the fire in his London home.

Sibyl Vane, the foolish young actress who preferred the eternity of death to living a life without her "Prince Charming." It astonished him that anyone could be so naïve as to construct a future on such a precarious foundation as love. Yet this was what she had done, only to fall to Dorian's feet and beg his forgiveness after performing woodenly on the stage and embarrassing him in front of his friends—in front of Lord Henry, no less! How could he have believed she had talent? Her only talent lay in the creation of art by the act of committing suicide. For that solitary performance

Dorian could at least find some admiration for her. He had been momentarily blinded by her comeliness—nay, he no longer thought of her as beautiful. True beauty was reserved for the superior—such as himself. He understood this now.

Although Lord Henry and Basil Hallward had both concurred that she was a lovely creature, it had not been enough to keep them there for the entirety of her excruciating performance as Shakespeare's Juliet. Instead they'd left Dorian sitting in his tawdry box in the tawdry theater surrounded by the unwashed stink of the rabble of London's underbelly, watching the play through to the very end, by which time he realized he needed to extricate himself from any romantic entanglement with Sibyl Vane. Indeed, his heart had broken as he watched her degrade herself upon the stage; then he felt nothing but the desire to be free of her. She had murdered his love as surely as she had murdered the role of Juliet. Regardless of her explanations—her claims that she no longer required the falseness of the stage with its artificial trappings now that she had *love*—Dorian's ears remained deaf to her.

That night, upon returning home from the theater, he had noticed the first sign of his portrait's alteration. An ugly cruelty now marred his perfect countenance—and it frightened him into repentance. Dorian decided that he would make amends to the actress and, indeed, marry her if this was what it took to earn redemption.

The next day Sibyl Vane was dead by her own hand.

That had been the first of many changes his portrait would undergo until he stored it beneath the ground, where he hoped never to set eyes upon it again. Dorian convinced himself that the actress's suicide had been the act of a weak-minded and foolish girl—a drama of far more consequence than her poor performance on the stage of a cut-rate London theater. It was nothing to do with him. He'd been blinded by her in the beginning, when he too was weak-minded and foolish. Such human foibles were behind him now. Sibyl Vane amounted to nothing more than a tiny pebble on a beach filled with tiny pebbles, none of any more significance than another. Her life, her *death*, held no value for him. This harsh realization marked the moment when Dorian felt himself change in earnest and all that remained of his innocence fade away.

Like Sibyl Vane, it would not be missed.

Dorian's life in Paris was filled with the promise of new sensations; he vowed to experience them all. Although this was not his first time in the city, it *was* his first time as the resurrected Dorian Gray, a gentleman of means whose wealth had been dispatched to various locations throughout the world. He continued to function using his real name, deeming it unlikely anyone should link him with the Dorian Gray who'd died tragically in a fire at his London home. The Englishman of the striking blue eyes and arresting countenance residing in Montparnasse was far too young to be connected to that unfortunate fellow who, by coincidence, shared the same name. Dorian now traveled in a very different society to that of London; the discovery of his true identity posed little risk.

The pleasures in the City of Light were endless. Sipping absinthe at Les Deux Magots and champagne at La Coupole; dining on an unpretentious meal of *choucroute garnie* at La Rotonde; listening to lively jazz music at Bricktop's... And the people who inhabited this remarkable city! Artists and writers from as far away as America became Dorian's regular companions—people whose names were on the lips of anyone who mattered. Although he was neither an artist nor a painter nor really much of anything but a pretty ornament, they welcomed him into their circle with open arms, his astonishing beauty the only calling card he required.

It was rumored that one of his friends—an American author notorious for his hard drinking and countless infidelities—had patterned a character in his novel after Dorian, though the fellow refused to acknowledge the veracity of the claim. It was also rumored that he had become Dorian's lover for a time, though this too was never acknowledged openly. The fact that the author had been spied leaving Dorian's apartment at an hour of the morning when one simply did not entertain guests gave the rumor more credence, as did the author's wife, who had a good deal to say on the subject to anyone with a willing ear. "My husband the sodomite," she was heard to call him whenever her tongue was loosened by liquor. Everyone suspected it was more from jealousy than marital possessiveness, since the wife too desired the young Englishman. As for Dorian, he neither confirmed nor denied the rumors that had placed him in a novel *and* in the arms of the gentleman who'd penned it. Although he couldn't be certain whether he had truly been the inspiration for a literary character, he did know with certainty that its author had occupied his bed—and done so without a moment's hesitation.

These were heady times for Dorian Gray. Intellectual discourse about art, literature, music and fashion took place long into the night at his apartment in Montparnasse, where the drink was always plentiful, as were the opportunities for pleasure. Unlike many of his artistic companions who struggled to pay the rent, Dorian had the means to be generous; therefore it was not surprising that his lodgings became a hub of social activity. It was during these occasions when he most poignantly felt Lord Henry Wotton's absence. How dear Harry would have thrived in such an atmosphere! No doubt many with whom Dorian was now acquainted would not have looked at all askance at Lord Henry's hedonistic philosophies, unlike their more prosaic London friends. On the contrary, they would have embraced them and lived them in earnest.

Sometimes when Dorian closed his eyes he could smell the opium-laced cigarettes his friend had smoked, then—upon re-opening them—see the blue wreathes of smoke spiraling upward, clouding the air. The experience was disorienting, especially when he realized that Lord Henry wasn't there in the room. His hands had been the white of lilies, each movement of the cigarette to his lips a performance of the utmost grace that even in memory still sparked chaos in Dorian's loins. Had circumstances been different, might they have become lovers? Surely the hedonism of which Lord Henry always spoke would have extended to the pursuit of fleshly pleasures between two men. There had been moments that passed between them—moments filled with a tension and intimacy that made Dorian believe it was possible. This had been the one thing Dorian regretted most in his life—not to have experienced the physical delights of his mentor. He would never forget Lord Henry's words to him: "Yes, Dorian, you will always be fond of me. I represent to you all the sins you have never had the courage to commit." But Harry had been wrong. Although he'd not been blind to Dorian's excesses, they had been minor in comparison to those to come.

Paris was the perfect city in which to live for the senses. Dorian's life here was far more exciting and decadent than anything he'd experienced at the seaside villa he had once shared with Lord Henry in Trouville—and they had considered themselves quite the connoisseurs of debauchery back then! Of course times had since become more liberal, thanks to the free-thinking attitude fostered by the presence of so many diverse artistic personalities. Although Dorian occasionally entertained the idea of seeing Trouville again, he had no way of knowing whether Lord Henry might still be frequenting the place, providing he was even alive. Despite his affection for the gentleman, Dorian dared not risk encountering him. He could trust no one; Basil Hallward had taught him that lesson.

Why had Hallward felt the need to meddle in Dorian's private affairs by coming to his home on that fog-shrouded eve of his thirty-eighth birthday? If the artist had kept his nose out of Dorian's business he might have lived to enjoy a ripe old age—and Dorian's hands would not be stained with his blood. "Anyone tormented by the guilt of murder will seek refuge in the grave; let no one hold them back," the Bible said. But Dorian wasn't tormented by guilt, and he had no desire to seek refuge in the grave. He had merely done what was necessary in order to save himself. Had Lord Henry been in his shoes he would probably have done the same. Dorian had been given no choice, not if he wished to continue with his life.

"Sin is the thing that writes itself across a man's face. It cannot be concealed," Hallward had told him that evening, at first softening the blow that he believed nothing that was being said about his young friend, only to next offer condemnation of Dorian's reported behavior, calling forth the rumors circulating about him as well as the names of those whose lives he'd ruined by his close association with them—names of both women *and* men, for Dorian had never discriminated when it came to gender. Although none of the artist's assertions were false, his chastisement had been sufficiently irksome that Dorian decided to take him upstairs to the old schoolroom to view his great work of art—to *see* his friend Dorian Gray as he truly was, his every sin laid bare on canvas. Hallward's reaction was as expected; when he begged the younger man to repent and pray with him, it was as if he had pulled a lever in Dorian's brain.

Dorian took up a knife and stabbed Basil Hallward until he was nothing but a pulp of bloodied flesh.

Indeed, perhaps those in the past were best left there, including Lord Henry Wotton. Dorian dwelled in the present, where his mind had the pleasure of consorting with the city's finest creative intellects and his body the pleasure of consorting with those who lived without inhibition; often the two were the same. As his relationship with the American author began to wane—a circumstance resulting from the fellow's excessive use of alcohol, which hampered his ability to perform, not from any falling-out between them—the void was filled by the author's wife. She too, was a writer from America, though terribly overshadowed by her husband. The couple's literary rivalry provided much fodder for gossip on both sides of the Atlantic. Dorian quite relished the idea of taking up with the wife when the husband's failings in the bedroom became too tedious to bear; he'd always found participating in a husband's cuckoldry to be an enjoyable enterprise and didn't mind in the least being used in this way.

An attractive young woman in her own right, she had adopted the style of *la garçonne*—a charming, androgynous look that extended beyond hair, makeup, and clothing to the bedroom. Such free-spirited young ladies, led by the author's wife, became Dorian's companions in bed—often several at a time. It became commonplace for these "flappers" to mount him one after the other, riding him until the seed erupted from his loins, at which point one would dismount and offer him to the next until all the young ladies had been serviced. That Dorian had the capacity to carry on despite the constant depletion of his resources was something he attributed to his perpetual state of youth, for which he had his accursed portrait to thank. Rather than diminishing with the years, his sexual stamina had increased, as did his appetites for all things related to the flesh.

Dorian's reputation as a libertine made him highly sought after by both women and men. It also made him a target for various intrigues, such as the one he now found himself in the midst of. As he would soon discover, the motives of a wife eclipsed in literature and in bed by her husband was a wife with more on her mind than her own physical pleasure.

"Next time I want him to be here," she told Dorian one night, the expression on her pretty features slightly demented. The other young ladies had by this time gone home; it was just the two of them, lying in Dorian's crumpled, sex-stained bed with their arms linked together, sharing a cigarette and staring up at the peeling paint on the ceiling, the smell of burning tobacco mingling with the smell of stale arousal.

"To be here for what?" he asked. "Your husband's cock is worth very little these days."

"I'm perfectly aware of that, Dorian. I've lived with it for years."

"Then why should you wish him to be present?"

"To watch you fuck me."

Dorian smiled, not taking her seriously. Although delightful in their open and brash manner, he'd concluded that the Americans too often tended toward exaggeration, uttering pronouncements they could not fulfill. Few of his acquaintances, American or other, enjoyed playing these dangerous games—and he didn't believe this neglected wife and scribe to be among them. "Are you not fanning a fire, my dear? Your husband's temper is such that most do not desire to be on the wrong side of it," he replied sensibly. Although the last thing Dorian feared was the gentleman's temper, the thought of sending the self-important fellow into a blind rage sounded like an amusing prospect. He found himself warming to the idea.

"That's why I want him to be here—to make him angry." Extricating her arm from Dorian's, she shifted position until her face hovered above his lap, whereupon she gave his still-erect flesh an extravagant lick with her tongue, leaving a smear of her recently reapplied lip rouge on the crown. Looking up at him with innocent eyes, she said: "I want to make him angry enough to spit fire."

Dorian had his doubts that what she was proposing would be sufficient as it now stood. Dorian as the only man in a bed filled with women—even if one of these women happened to be the author's wife—did not sound as if it would spark the flame that was required. In fact, the fellow to whom this performance was directed might find it very much to his liking, since he would then have the bodies of many other appealing females to admire. He believed they required an additional player for their game, and he had the perfect candidate—another American writer in their circle with a fondness for hard living. He had a rugged masculine appearance usually reserved for men who'd accumulated many more years of life, though this did not detract from his appeal. "Leave it with me," said Dorian, leaning in for a kiss. His companion's lips tasted of tobacco, gin, and women, which wasn't surprising considering she'd just spent the best part of the evening with her mouth between the thighs of their female bed partners.

The following morning Dorian put the plan into motion.

That evening the two gentlemen authors arrived at Dorian's Montparnasse apartment, one believing that he would be enjoying an evening of drink and cards without the nagging presence of his wife, the other knowing that he had been called here for a different purpose entirely. The first discovered his wife laid out like a sacrificial lamb on Dorian's bed along with several other young ladies, all of them in a similar state of undress. Although this tableau of female flesh was not in any way objectionable, he had *not* expected to find Dorian or his literary cohort located among them, also without benefit of clothing. The former's body was beautifully crafted and the author experienced a flush of pride that he had come to know it so intimately, but the other man possessed the stockiness of a farmhand, making the thought of such intimacy repellent to him.

At first the husband took matters in stride, deciding to avail himself of the excellent bottle of whiskey Dorian had thoughtfully provided. He watched from a chair as the young ladies took turns atop his host, whose stamina for the act never waned. Unfortunately, it served to remind the author of his own recent inadequacies in this area, prompting the contents of the bottle to be reduced with increasing speed. His friend likewise benefitted as the women climbed atop him as well, though it gave the author some satisfaction to note that he required a period of recovery between each. He also took satisfaction in the fact that his wife remained a passive observer. Although irritated that she was naked in front of the two men, he decided it wasn't worth getting into a temper about, since all she seemed to be doing was watching and occasionally touching between her thighs, as if uncertain how to go about it. Clearly she was as inept at self-pleasure as she was at writing. Although tempted to order her from the room, he thought it best to say nothing. "Better to remain silent and be thought a fool then to speak out and remove all doubt," as the great American president Abraham Lincoln had once said.

Chuckling at his wife's pitiful attempts to pleasure herself, he swallowed down the remainder of the whiskey in his glass, the burn going directly to his belly and igniting a fire of desire in his loins that been sadly absent for some time. Although his desire was more for that damnable opening located between the rear cheeks of the Englishman than for any belonging to the ladies present, he refused to give in—not with his wife and the other author in the room. Yet how he longed to have him again; it had been like sliding into a tube of heated silk. Tamping down his need, he located another bottle from which to drink until his eyes intersected and the figures on the bed had doubled in number. He nearly toppled over right where he sat, managing to catch himself before he made a fool of himself and fell to the floor.

Refocusing his attention on the bed, he discovered that his wife had relinquished her post as passive observer and was lying beneath Dorian, her calves draped on his shoulders as he entered her. Why, only a moment ago Gray had been inside another woman and now here he was, thrusting that herculean organ of his into the Southern belle he'd married! He could feel rage bubbling up in his throat, along with the whiskey he'd consumed, until he feared he would disgrace himself all over his shirtfront and trousers. His wife cried out with a pleasure he had never been able to coax from her, not even when they still retained the ecstatic flush of newlyweds.

Before he had fully absorbed the sordid reality of what was happening, his author friend replaced Dorian and proceeded to plow into his wife's dainty opening with all the finesse of a tractor. She moaned and writhed beneath him, crying out his name with a passion the likes of which he'd never heard in their own bed. Her performance was no pretense. The woman was genuinely enjoying herself, her nails drawing trails of blood down the fellow's wide back until it looked as though he'd been in a fight with a wildcat. If this wasn't insult enough, she grabbed hold of Dorian's erect flesh, her small fist working it toward fruition.

The taste of insanity was sour on his tongue. He

could not allow this to go on! Pushing himself up from his chair, he staggered forward as he considered who among the three he would kill first—his wife, the Englishman, or his fellow expatriate from America. "No!" he shouted, his deep voice booming against the walls, disturbing no one but the young ladies who'd been left wanting at the sidelines. He grabbed the empty whiskey bottle and smashed it into the side of the table. He was left holding the neck, which terminated in a fringe of jagged glass that would be excellent for slicing through the throats of two men and one woman. Willing himself forward to the bed, he discovered that he could not move; it was as if the soles of his shoes had been glued to the floorboards.

If the featured players on the stage were aware that they'd become the intended objects of murder, they seemed impervious to it. Once again the wife of the author found herself beneath Dorian as he resumed his attentions, the rawness of her moans continuing to torment her husband's ears. To Dorian's delight, the rugged gentleman whom he had replaced positioned himself at his backside and entered him hard—so hard it stole the breath from his lungs. With every primitive thrust he received, Dorian was forced deeper into the woman, the three of them moving together in a vulgar ballet that made its drunken observer fear he had finally lost his mind. He fell backward into his chair, where he promptly lost consciousness.

Although Dorian continued to encounter the American couple socially along with their friend, the events of that night were never mentioned. He did note that the wife appeared to be of a far sunnier disposition of late and had even begun work on a new novel, whereas her husband complained incessantly of suffering from a malady he referred to as "writer's block." Dorian began to find the self-absorption of his literary companions rather tiresome, along with the marital one-upmanship. He was also growing bored with the boyish allure of *la garçonne*. Like all amusements, they grew stale after a while, leaving one wanting. He desired more unsavory games, where the players were not those with whom he associated but those from society's lower ranks. Therefore when a gentleman in his social circle—an artist with a reputation for any number of colorful vices—recommended to him one of the city's more illustrious brothels, Dorian hesitated not a moment.

Although such establishments were not unknown to him, the one to which he was directed catered to the upper classes. It bore scant resemblance to the foul dens and unsavory taverns Dorian had known back in London, which teemed with women who had coarse faces and even coarser manners. Indeed, he had dwelled in the gutter and adored it. But like everything else, he'd become weary of this too, moving from the pigsties at the docks to the calculated corruption of those with whom he associated in society, despoiling a number of fine young men until they'd either taken their own lives in shame or joined the gutter-dwellers and become no better than the pox-ridden whores at the docks. Every accusation Basil Hallward had flung at him on his final night of life had been correct, as were the names of those whose lives he'd ruined.

Dorian cut his eye teeth at Un Deux Deux, one of Paris's most famous brothels, before his inevitable boredom forced him to seek out houses with a reputation for encouraging more unsavory pursuits. Aside from having exhausted what was on offer, there was a more pressing reason for Dorian's decision to take his business to another establishment: his past appeared to be catching up with him. One evening while leaving Un Deux Deux, he heard the madam greet by name some old friends of his from London—Lord Gerald and Lady Priscilla Oadby. That they could be the same Lord and Lady Oadby from Connaught Square with whom he'd often cavorted caused a prickle of fear to run down his spine. Until this moment he had happened upon no one from his previous life; he'd allowed himself to become complacent in the belief that he never would. Surely by now he had outlived nearly everyone, especially those owning as many years as the Oadbys!

The couple was the typical sort with whom he and Lord Henry had associated—wealthy and idle. Not surprisingly, they had taken an instant liking to Dorian not only for his exceptional beauty but also for his penchant for indulging in any number of decadences. He had passed many nights of fleshly recreation with the Oadbys before his "death." Under different circumstances he would have been pleased to renew the acquaintance, even if merely to reminisce over a bottle of wine. But his circumstances were now such that a meeting between them would have been extremely unwise. These were not people who could easily keep a confidence.

On hearing their names, Dorian hazarded a glance into the parlor, taking note of the side view of an elderly couple in the company of a very tall and slender young lady who looked more male than female. Were it not for the revealing décolletage of her bodice, he might have mistaken her for a man. As the madam moved to join the party, the couple turned in his direction.

Dorian heard the shattering of glass and realized the sound was in his mind. It was the sound of recognition. His first instinct was to run up and greet the Oadbys like the old friends they were, but his youthful appearance juxtaposed against their timeworn versions gave him cause for alarm, as did the fact that all of London believed him to be dead. Seeing Dorian Gray alive and looking as handsome and young as the first day they'd met would give rise to speculation that could destroy the new life he'd created for himself in Paris. Hoping they had not seen him, he fled into the night, certain that he would never return to this place again.

Had Dorian chosen to remain behind for a moment longer, he might have seen the shock that had registered on the Oadbys' faces. The couple had, indeed, glimpsed their old friend from London and, though the view had been brief, he had looked remarkably unchanged from the last time they'd set eyes on his perfect visage. Rumors of the resurrected Dorian Gray soon began to circulate among their British associates in Paris, eventually traveling across the Channel via letter to Curzon Street, Mayfair, where it reached the aged ear of Lord Henry Wotton. Though believing none of it, he still dared to hope that the stories of his friend's rebirth might be true. Lord Henry was nearing the end of his life, but to know that Dorian was alive and well and as exquisitely perfect as he had been on that fateful afternoon they'd first met in Basil Hallward's studio would have made him ready to accept death.

Dorian knew nothing of this at the time, his companions in society being wholly unconnected to the Oadbys'. Having by now quit the sphere of his self-obsessed American literary companions, he had begun to spend more time with the Spanish artist he had met through these very same people. The odd little fellow proved to be a wellspring of information on the brothels of Paris, having already recommended Un Deux Deux, and Dorian soon learned of another establishment run by a Madame Cherie. "She is utterly delightful!" proclaimed the artist, his thumb and forefinger twisting the curled-up ends of his long black mustache with glee. "You will find her most accommodating of a gentleman's particular...*needs*." Of this Dorian had no doubt, for the Spaniard had a reputation for engaging in some rather curious practices that had resulted in his being banned from several brothels. The fact that Dorian's *needs* were growing increasingly base encouraged him to give Madame Cherie's a try.

The establishment was conveniently situated within the same arrondissement in which Dorian kept his apartment. Although not as notable as Un Deux Deux, what the house lacked in fame it made up for in variety. According to his artist friend, Madame Cherie's boasted a pair of hermaphrodites, each of whom—or so it was rumored—had the working parts of both genders. "You must sample them in turn, then report back to me as to which of them you preferred. I wish to hear every detail!" he instructed, making no attempt to hide the protrusion denting his trouser front. Dorian almost expected him to display himself in hopes that his audience might find the cause of the disturbance to his liking and decide to do something about it.

The artist's notorious fondness for absinthe had been the catalyst for far more inspirational pursuits than taking a brush to canvas. It was one of the qualities that had made his companionship so useful to Dorian—

he suffered from no lack of inhibition and was always willing to share his knowledge as to which perversions could be found where. He knew every unsavory nook and cranny in Paris, particularly those featuring activities of a more disreputable nature. Although Dorian had developed a fondness for the curious little Spaniard and considered his paintings of giant heads and melting clocks rather extraordinary, his fondness did not extend beyond the confines of friendly conversation and a shared love of *la fée verte.*

Recalling the Oadbys' strange companion at Un Deux Deux, Dorian concluded that hermaphroditism must be quite the rage in Paris. Had he not wished to keep his presence from them a secret, he might have introduced the couple to the artist. He felt certain they would have become fast friends, the Oadbys always having had an appreciation of the bizarre. He still remembered the party of male dwarves they had engaged to entertain them in their bedroom, one of whom had collapsed in exhaustion.

As for the pair of hermaphrodites, Dorian did not encounter them. Madame Cherie either kept them under lock and key for her long-term clients or they were a myth magnified to grand proportions by an artist's absinthe-soaked tongue. He was more inclined toward the latter explanation; in addition to a fondness for the green liqueur, the Spaniard was also fond of opiates and was frequently known to speak of things that did not exist. Dorian would not have been surprised if the fellow had spoken of coupling with dragons. Perhaps it was no wonder his paintings contained such disturbing elements.

Dorian's increasing hunger for new sensation soon

overrode everything else, including his enjoyment of any form of society that did not contain physical pleasure. Dispensing with intellectualism and social companionship, he focused exclusively on matters of the flesh. It was as if he'd been turned into a starving man who—no matter how much he consumed—could not fill the vacancy in his belly. The nightly conversational soirees in his apartment were no more; instead his nights were spent between the thighs of ladies of the evening. Although securing the fleshly charms of women had never been difficult, Dorian had discovered that the majority of the gender—no matter how free-thinking they claimed to be—failed to possess the erotic imaginations and abilities of those professionally trained for it. These ladies were highly skilled in the art of physical love; they spent their every waking moment engaged in it. However, there were more practical benefits to their companionship. To take pleasure without worrying about such feminine nuisances as romance or ruffling delicate sensibilities or, even worse, *pregnancy* made the brothel a perfect solution for a gentleman who had all too often been forced to extricate himself from the tiresome clutches of women who fancied themselves in love. A recent confrontation in such a matter by the wife of the American author had been the deciding factor in Dorian's decision to pay for his pleasure rather than receive it for free.

The encounter had taken place at Chez Bricktop, where he had gone to refresh himself with a pleasant evening of drink and jazz. The evening did not remain pleasant for long. She was seated at a table near the musicians, drinking heavily; from the state of her it looked as if she had been doing so for some time. Tension radiated like waves from her body, indicating that an explosion was imminent. The woman was frequently prone to outbursts and many regarded her as not entirely stable. Dorian saw no sign of her husband, who was a regular patron at the club, though he did recognize the gentleman accompanying her—an American poet with a fondness for spelling his name in lowercase letters.

Dorian had been engaged in conversation over a cigar with Ada, the club's owner and performer, when he heard his name being shouted from across the room. There could be no mistaking the Southern-belle accent of the woman endeavoring to gain his attention. He tried to blend in with a cluster of people standing nearby swaying to the music, but she wouldn't be dissuaded. "Dorian!" she cried, her shrill voice drowning out the lively music and garnering a scowl from the bass player. She began waving her hands about in the air. Dorian had no choice but to acknowledge her—and he did so with an inclination of his head and a polite smile, for by then even the poet was staring in his direction. He hoped the acknowledgement would be sufficient to satisfy her.

"*Dorian!*"

It appeared he had no choice but to join her table. No sooner had he lowered himself into a chair than she grabbed his hand in both of hers, holding it in a vice. "Where have you been? Why haven't you been to see me?" Her voice was that of a shrew nagging a henpecked husband. "I called at your apartment three times last week! Didn't you get my note?"

The note, which had contained a demand that they meet, had been discarded the instant after Dorian had read it. "Note?" he asked, all innocence.

"I left it at your door!"

"Perhaps a gust of wind blew it away."

"A *gust of wind*?" She laughed loudly, eliciting yet another scowl from the bass player. "Oh, you silly boy! How very droll!" Considering that Dorian's front door was located *inside* the building rather than facing onto a street or courtyard, he too, saw the humor of the situation. Suddenly she stopped laughing. "Dorian, I absolutely must speak to you!"

"But my dear, you are speaking to me now."

Her mouth twisted into an ugly red grimace. "That is *not* what I meant!"

Dorian could see that she was becoming annoyed and it pleased him that he seemed to be the cause of it. Perhaps she wished to enlist him for another of her little revenge games against her husband. If so, he had no desire to play. He had enjoyed it at the time, particularly the final act in which he had been the receiver as well as the giver, but he had since moved on to other, far less complicated diversions.

"Dorian, I am carrying your child!"

The words detonated like a bomb; that half the room had overheard them made the impact even worse. The poet's expression alternated between embarrassment and amusement, as if it couldn't decide which emotion best suited the situation. It eventually settled on embarrassment.

"Did you not hear me?" She was screaming now, her eyes wide and deranged. The poet looked ready to flee the table, as did a number of people from neighboring tables.

"My dear lady, everyone in this establishment heard you. In fact, they probably heard you on the other side of the river." Dorian dragged his hand out from her grasp and stood up. "I request that you do not speak to me or come to my home again. I wish to have nothing more to do with you." With those parting words, he left the nightclub—and with it, the last contact he would ever have with Paris's expatriate literary society.

She had lied, of course. Dorian had spied her a few months later with her husband at a café on the Place Pigalle. He had detected no evidence of a swollen belly. On the contrary, she looked thinner, as if she had not been eating, her eyes even more unhinged than the night he'd seen her at Bricktop's. As for her husband, his face had developed the heavy jowls of a man who drinks to excess. Dorian hurried away before either of them saw him.

He'd had enough of the dramas of women. From now on he would seek them out in brothels, where their relationships would terminate after payment had been rendered.

It was at Madame Cherie's where Dorian eventually came to meet Celestine. Only gentlemen of means were able to afford access to her charms, thereby increasing her exclusivity. Like others who possessed an abundance of it, Dorian considered money to be a coarse topic of conversation; since he had plenty to spare, he wasn't about to quibble over a few francs. He was happy to pay the price demanded of him, for Celestine was a lovely creature with lively green eyes and a delightfully compliant temperament. Her lips were the pink of newly unfurled rose petals and equally as silken. Indeed, it was the sweet pout of her mouth that commanded the princely sum set by the house. It was impossible to imagine those virginal lips opening to receive the greedy flesh of a man, and yet this had become the principal function for which Celestine was celebrated. Having been pleasured in this manner by any number of women, Dorian had been skeptical that she could live up to her reputation. The large sum he was required to put forth in advance to Madame Cherie was extortionary—so much so that he wondered if he were being swindled. He had heard of several gentlemen with wealth that exceeded even his own who had struggled to pay the amount, but Madame Cherie was unyielding in the policies of the house. "A gentleman's pedigree does not entitle him to discounts," the plain-speaking madam could often be heard to remark, her chastisement prompting a number of these gentlemen's countenances to heighten with embarrassment.

Perhaps he should have been kinder to Celestine. But kindness was for the weak and the inferior—and Dorian Gray was neither. He had not been granted the gift of eternal youth and beauty in order to bestow kindness upon those less fortunate than himself. Lord Henry Wotton had taught him well.

Having paid his money and then some, Dorian took Celestine in every manner there was in which to take a woman, yet still he was not satisfied. His hunger for sensation swelled within him like an inflating balloon. It was as if a form of madness had taken hold. He wondered if it were possible to catch madness like a disease; if so, he had surely been infected by the American writer's wife. Rumors had since reached his ear that she'd returned to her home country, where she was now ensconced in a sanitarium. Apparently he no longer needed to be concerned about encountering her again or being the object of her deranged accusations, though he couldn't help but suspect that her husband had had a hand in her institutionalization.

Dorian called in every night at Madame Cherie's, where Celestine waited in a lavishly appointed bedroom whose splendor paled if one turned up the lights too brightly. Her splendor, however, did not pale, nor did her guise of innocence. She was a charming little creature who virtually begged to be used and controlled. Dorian suspected these qualities had more to do with her true nature than with any amount of money he was paying for her services. Having paid his pound of flesh, he used her mouth with impunity, along with the mouth of her sex and the more illicit mouth for which the price was dearer, enjoying her squeals and protestations as she tried to wriggle out of his grasp. When he grew bored, he bound her limbs with the silken cords from the draperies, fastening them to the iron posts of her bed.

"Monsieur Gray, you are so terribly wicked!" cried Celestine as he rendered her immobile.

Dorian erupted with laughter at her response. That his desires had become progressively unconventional since his "death" was something he eagerly embraced. He wanted to experience all that life had to offer—and the more forbidden and degenerate, the better. Had he the ability to see into the future, he might have acted with more caution, for a life totally absent of restraint eventually led to bedlam.

The fact that he could shock one of her ilk was especially gratifying. One might have imagined that a *prostituée*—nay, a *putain*—had seen and experienced it all, but clearly not. Dorian had no patience for semantics. In his mind a whore was a whore—setting a high tariff on one did not alter the label. He soon took to calling Celestine his "little whore," a soubriquet she came to adopt when referring to herself in conversation with him. He assumed it was done to please him and to earn herself a more generous gratuity. He hadn't realized it was done out of love. Indeed, Celestine had lost her heart to the beautiful and perfect Dorian Gray. Although this should not have come as a surprise, he was genuinely unaware of it, interpreting her every action to please him as yet another attempt to remove money from his pocket.

Having become bored with play, Dorian pushed her face into the satin pillow, since his needs had not as yet been met. The young woman knew well the difficulty of accommodating her demanding client in the less traditional fashion and struggled in her bonds. Madame Cherie had already required Dorian to pay extra money to the house each time his special desires had rendered Celestine unable to work for several days, even going so far as to suggest that he might avail himself of one of the other ladies who were more fluent in these practices and therefore more accommodating to a well-endowed gentleman such as himself. However, Dorian remained unmoved by the madam's obvious attempts at flattery and subterfuge. He only wanted Celestine. The desire to spoil her for anyone else was like an exotic sweet on his tongue.

This evening she was being particularly difficult, her backside rearing up like a horse bucking to shift its rider, the effort designed more so to encourage rather than dissuade him. Dorian was aware that the enjoyment to be gained was not one-sided; when he reached beneath her to touch her sex, he found it as expected. Using the wetness to prepare her, he moved the tip of his erection into place and began to press forward. Suddenly Celestine went quiet, as if her tongue, too, had been forced into submission.

"My lovely little whore, your body never lies to me," Dorian whispered into the dainty swirls of her ear. He felt her interior clench in response and knew that her battle had, indeed, been yet another artifice designed to put coins into her purse. He couldn't altogether blame her. In all likelihood Madame Cherie paid the young ladies in her employ a pittance of what she took in for their services. Perhaps he would be extra generous tonight and leave Celestine with an amount equivalent to the pleasure she provided, though he'd make certain that she earned it.

Dorian spent himself once, only to continue without cease, working toward his second climax as Celestine's passions pulsed hotly against his immersed flesh. Just as the pressure in his testes became too much to bear, he heard a muffled cry from below. It was followed by his own as he released himself inside her. Hot tears flowed in salty rivulets down Celestine's pleasure-flushed cheeks, leaving pale tracks through the rouge painted on her cheeks. Had Dorian seen them, he might have mistook them for tears of suffering rather than what they truly were—for by then Celestine's feelings were such that she believed she could not live without him.

Dorian continued to visit Celestine over the years, though with decreasing frequency—at most twice weekly and only then to indulge in the more base of practices, one of which she repeatedly refused. Her supple body began to display signs of decay. At first it manifested around the eyes by means of a series of fine lines that etched themselves deeper over time, eventually progressing to a slackening of the breasts, belly, and buttocks. He noted that the other ladies in Madame Cherie's employment had taken on similar characteristics, though like Celestine they were still prepossessing enough to work, albeit fewer hours, as younger and less timeworn versions joined the house and drew in the wealthier clients.

That Dorian seemed to be the only one who hadn't aged did not go unnoticed. Madame Cherie remarked to him one evening: "Monsieur Gray, you are as young and handsome today as you were when you first came to me, yet I have become an old woman! How can this be?"

If Madame Cherie had noticed how unchanged he was, it stood to reason others had as well. The time had come to quit his patronage of her establishment and, indeed, quit Montparnasse altogether.

Dorian made arrangements to take an apartment in another, less popular arrondissement, so as to lessen the chances of encountering Madame Cherie or anyone else from her establishment—particularly Celestine, who no longer possessed the charms he'd once enjoyed. He need not have concerned himself, however; he later learned that she had cut her wrists after he'd stopped coming to see her. The letter she had written to Dorian was delivered to his Montparnasse apartment a week after her death and the day before he was to vacate the premises. It had gone unnoticed on the table at Madame Cherie's front door by the boy who ran errands for the house. Rather than own his role in the letter's delay, the lad had merely delivered it to its intended recipient, either unaware or unconcerned that its author was by that time dead.

Mon cher Dorian,

Why do you not come to see me? Have I done something to displease you? Pray, tell me what it is that I have done and allow me to make it up to you! There is nothing I would not do for you. Nothing!

Have you grown tired of me, my beloved? Is it because I would not do that one thing you asked me to do? But cher, il n'est pas possible! None of the ladies here has allowed a man to do this and I'm certain Madame Cherie would most heartily forbid it! Oh, I realize that it can be a secret between us only—she need never know.

Does it truly mean so much to you, my darling? If so, I shall bear it. I shall bear it for you. I shall bear the pain and the humiliation of it, if it pleases you and gives you pleasure. For I live only to give you pleasure and make you happy! I hope then that you will comprehend the depths of my love for you.

There. I have said it. I have agreed! You have it in writing, a binding agreement should you wish to take me to the courts. Let it happen soonest so that you can reap the reward. How I shall enjoy seeing your face when the pleasure of it overtakes you! Quickly, let us do this deed tonight! I will make the preparations so that everything is ready for your arrival. And I will speak of it to no one. No one.

Let me close this letter by saying this, my

beautiful Dorian. I cannot go on without you. It has already been too long since our last meeting and my heart aches grievously, as does my body for the absence of yours. If you do not come to me tonight, I will know it is because you no longer desire to.

If you do not appear in my room by midnight, I shall have no remedy but to quit this life forever. May my blood be upon your hands.

With all my love,
Your petite Celestine
(Your little whore)

Dorian crumpled up the letter and threw it into the fire, watching dispassionately as the flames ate the delicate lilac notepaper. Had it been delivered on the day its author had intended, it would have made no difference.

The curse of Sibyl Vane still hung upon him like a shroud—a shroud he was destined never to cast off.

Dorian's Paris had begun to change. As he returned to the places he'd once frequented, he noticed that he no longer appeared to be the golden boy everyone adored. It eventually became impossible for him not to notice the stares or overhear the whispers of those in society as he dined at the city's cafés or visited its nightclubs or strolled along its avenues. At first he attributed this to nothing more than the ruffled egos of those for whom he no longer had time, but eventually he sensed that something more was at hand. It brought back memories of his days in London, when invitations were no longer forthcoming and the doors to all the best residences shut to him. Other than dear Harry, Lord and Lady Oadby had been the only ones who continued to consort openly with him, without concern for being tainted by association. Although it had been some time since their near-encounter, Dorian wondered if the Oadbys might still be in Paris—if so, had they perchance seen him? He knew that wagging tongues could do great damage—and it was obvious by the dramatically changed attitudes toward him that tongues had indeed been wagging.

Yet Dorian's shunning was nothing in comparison to the mounting tension permeating the streets and alleyways of Paris like a bad stink. It hung over the shoulders of the populace, a poisonous pong filling the mouth and nostrils and crawling down the throat until it became impossible to breathe. Men, women, and children were constantly glancing over their shoulders, as if expecting to see a sinister figure ready to slit their throats with a blade. This new sense of fear casting a shadow over the city was not entirely unfounded; Dorian had noted the increasing presence of German soldiers on the streets and in the bars and cafés, their hard pale faces never smiling, their hard pale eyes glinting with a sadistic cruelty the world had never before experienced but would speak of for generations to come. The City of Light was fading.

It was time for Dorian to move on.

MARRAKESH,
194—

The only difference between a caprice and a lifelong passion is that the caprice lasts a little longer.

—LORD HENRY WOTTON

Dorian sat at his favorite outdoor café in Djemaa El Fna Square, drinking a cup of fragrant tea delivered on a hammered-gold tray. He displayed all the leisure of a man with no pressing need to be anywhere else—and, indeed, he had no such need. Life in this desert oasis was filled with ease and relaxation, suiting him in a way that London and Paris never had. The afternoon call to prayer had begun; it was a quiet time of the day, as the devout filled the mosques or set down their prayer mats where they stood. Even the merchants in the souk had dropped to their knees to bow toward Mecca.

He had expected to pine for Paris like a sentimental lover. Instead, Marrakesh cured him of it. Here Dorian could start afresh, far from the condemning eyes and gossiping tongues of people with nothing to occupy their time but engaging in idle speculation. Here he was unlikely to encounter his past—the Americans had all gone home to America to escape the war and the English were likely all dead. This was a place where he could reinvent himself.

In Morocco Dorian decided to live as a Moroccan. He walked the narrow winding streets dressed in loose native garments and bargained in the souks with the expertise of one born to it. Although money was of little consequence to him, haggling was expected—a merchant would be insulted if one did not participate in the negotiations. He'd even picked up a fair amount of Berber and Darija Arabic to supplement his French; they aided him well in his dealings. Although his fair features marked him as such, he no longer felt foreign. Flowing garments such as the gandora, worn with the turban or fez, were the mode of fashion in this city rather than the stiff hats and staid suits of the west, the latter of which singled out their wearers as foreigners even more than the shade of their skin. Adopting the style of the locals made Dorian feel remarkably free and unencumbered. He strove to live a more quiet existence than he was accustomed to, blending in as much as it was possible for a fair-skinned, blue-eyed Englishman to do. If he remained discreet in his activities, he should be able to pass many happy years in this part of the world.

The pleasures of the Red City proved infinitely

more exotic than those of European cities; Dorian had stopped in many before reaching North Africa, but found none captivated him enough to remain for very long. Even the moon seemed changed in this strange and ancient landscape, as though it had been fashioned from different elements. He could almost feel it calling to him. After bathing in rosewater and anointing himself with fragrant oils, Dorian would go up to the rooftop of his modest little walled-in house to watch it rise between the tall minarets of the mosque a few streets away, feeling a vibration going through him. It was the nearest he'd ever come to a religious experience; he considered himself godless, despite a former fascination for the trappings and ceremonies of the Roman Catholic Church. Indeed, no god would have granted him a life that had no end date—especially a life with no other purpose but sin, vice, and depravity.

Dorian had been drawn to the Sahara for its familiarity. He and Lord Henry had once shared a little walled-in house in Algiers. Yet the familiar often bred boredom, and it would not be long before the urge to seek out new sensations began to eat away at him like the pox eats away at the flesh, destroying his newfound contentment and sending him into the streets to search for forbidden pleasures. The hunger had never truly left him, but he had managed to keep it tamped down until very recently. This, though, was a new kind of hunger—a dark and debasing one that took him completely by surprise.

Dorian placed a brown cube of sugar upon his tongue and took a sip of hot, fragrant tea, allowing the cube to melt in his mouth. The sweetness spread throughout his body like a living thing, reaching every hidden corner of his being. Everything tasted sweeter here, even the air, some of which was richly scented with opium. Dorian's afternoon tea ritual was a simple pleasure in which he engaged at the same time each day at a café conveniently situated only a few minutes' walk from his house in the medina. The pace of this ancient North African city suited him. It was indolent and sinuous, with an undercurrent of the divinely sinister.

Thieves, villains, and thugs roamed Marrakesh, joining with well-heeled Westerners, snake charmers, and dervishes as the sun cast the city in hues of pink and gold and orange that deepened to red with the approach of nightfall. There were moments when the winding little streets and alleyways looked as if blood had been spilled in them—as perhaps it had. Intrigued by the city's more unsavory residents, Dorian's fascination prompted him to place himself in harm's way time and again as he sought to appease his hunger. Indeed, the genteel young gentleman drinking tea in the afternoon bore little resemblance to the lost soul begging for degradation in the night.

Dorian couldn't help noticing a man and woman a few tables away noticing *him*. The couple was well dressed, though obviously foreign and of an advanced age. Their features indicated that they might be English. They had probably come to Marrakesh seeking out warmer climes in their winter years, leaving the cold of England behind to amplify every ache and malady of those less fortunate than themselves.

Turning away his gaze, he gave them no more thought. Dorian was accustomed to being stared at; more often than not he found it amusing. To his delight, he discovered that each time he looked into a mirror he was more beautiful than ever. The face staring back at him hadn't changed since his portrait sitting in Basil Hallward's studio. It appeared that he wore sin and vice extremely well; he took comfort in the fact that their ravages were taking place on a canvas many thousands of miles away instead of on the image being reflected back to him.

Dorian derived great pleasure from standing unclothed before the tall mirror in his bedroom and savoring the perfect lines of his form. His passion rose as he admired himself from every conceivable angle, bending and twisting his body until there was no part remaining that he had not tasted with his eyes. His well-formed torso was pleasingly free of the clutter of hair as it tapered down to a trim waist that boasted a charming button of an umbilicus. The contours of his hips possessed enough curve to still be masculine without the boxiness of most males. They created a worthy frame for the appendage of flesh that rose upward from his loins with a princely pride he never tired of admiring. How he longed to drop to his knees and take it into his mouth as so many others had done, if only it had been possible to step outside his body to do so. To experience his own body as others had done—that would truly be something!

The frustration of his inability to worship at his own altar became an obsession that haunted Dorian's consciousness until he believed he would go mad with the desire to engage in self-love. This obsession was joined by still another each time he admired the perfect pair of cushions to the aft, the deep crease marking their separation triggering within him a powerful yearning to defile the secrets that lay within. He burned with an anguished need that not even he could name until finally he could no longer ignore it.

Dorian's period of contentment had come to an end.

These nightly rituals of self-admiration eventually led him to seek out the hard bodies of young males, hoping to find satisfaction for a desire for degradation so overwhelming there were moments when he did not recognize himself. Dorian knew that he must be cautious in his search, his adopted land being a dichotomy of the morally decadent and the spiritually devout. Although the former were plentiful in supply if one knew where to look, those in the latter category often maintained a suspicion of Westerners, especially those who flaunted themselves openly with no concern for social or cultural niceties. Dorian was not a fool. The penalties for such "perversions" included public stoning—or worse. Had he been discovered, being locked away inside a filthy cell might be the least of his concerns. Although money could buy his way out of many things, there were some in this part of the world whose moral values meant more than a fistful of bank notes.

In one of the opium dens he frequented, Dorian heard talk about alleyways in the poorer sections of the medina that offered exactly what he sought. Although the mumblings of a man in a poppy-induced haze were not necessarily the stuff of fact, he thought this as good a place as any to begin his quest. For several nights running Dorian visited the same alleyway, passing casually from one end to the other until he was certain beyond a doubt that the handsome young males gathered beneath the archway were there for one purpose. Perhaps it *had* been true what he'd overheard—one needed only to walk down the correct alleyway after nightfall and display the correct turn of countenance to locate a willing partner. The men recognized Dorian from his earlier expeditions just as he recognized many of them in return. Occasionally they called out a taunt, testing him—indeed, *daring* him to make an advance. Some were barely more than boys, but their aggressive stances belied any tendency toward innocence. These creatures were equally capable of sucking a man's cock or cutting his throat—and the danger of it all sent a frisson of excitement through Dorian that energized the barometer of his need until it tented the front of his gandora, providing confirmation to his onlookers as to his reasons for being here.

Yet he had not come to this alleyway for the services the bolder members of the group barked out to him. Those ready to drop to their knees or bend over for a few francs held no interest for Dorian. He didn't wish to lead the dance, but rather to be the one *led*—and for this only the most forceful among them would do. That he should now desire to strip away every component of his dominant masculinity and submit completely to the will of another of his sex—and do so to the point of physical and mental degradation—was an entirely new addition to his repertoire of sensation.

Dorian soon became quite expert at detecting that special glint of cruelty in these young males' hooded eyes that promised satisfaction for his dark urges. The first time it happened he found himself being led deeper into the alleyway, where in the shadows of another ancient archway he was pushed onto his knees. No sooner did they make contact with the cobbles than his mouth fell open like that of a worshipper awaiting Communion. Rather than the Host being placed upon his tongue, he received the heavy flesh of another man's sex, which would then be forced repeatedly down his throat with no regard for civility until it felt as if Dorian's back teeth had been knocked loose. His hair was seized by coarse fingers and twisted and pulled until his eyes brimmed, then overflowed, with tears. They spilled shamefully down his cheeks as he choked on the object filling his mouth, gagging and sputtering as jets of hot fluid hit the back of his throat. Rather than spitting out what he'd been made to take in, Dorian swallowed it as the other man stared down at him in contempt. His humiliation was complete—or so he believed, until he felt the leather toe of the young man's babouche connecting hard with his belly. It was followed by a hand searching the sides of his gandora until it located the hidden pocket, releasing from it the bank notes and coins he had brought with him tonight. Having found what he wanted, his assailant moved off to rejoin his companions. Suddenly Dorian heard them laughing and felt certain he was the object of their amusement. To his astonishment, he found that it pleased him; in all likelihood they had witnessed the entire episode.

Still doubled over from his assault, Dorian smiled up into the darkness, the movement causing his jaw to pain him grievously from the strain it had undergone. Not only was the young man brutal, he'd been extremely well endowed—indeed, nearly on a par with himself. The loss of a few bank notes and coins was of no matter; Dorian had intended to pay and believed he had received excellent value for his money. As he stood he noticed that the front of his garment was marked by something wet and sticky. So occupied had he been in the glories of his debasement that he hadn't even noticed the arrival of his own climax.

Dorian returned several times to the alleyway, reenacting the same scene with different players. Sometimes they came with a beating, other times not. The young men had already created their own nickname for the pale foreigner who foolishly thought that donning the native garb made him a Moroccan. They called him *pédéraste*. That they failed to apply the label to themselves was a form of hypocritical reasoning only the most blatantly masculine could comprehend. In their minds they were simply selling a service on a par with the old man at the souk who polished the leather shoes of spoiled foreigners.

Unbeknownst to them, Dorian had begun to frequent other alleyways as well. He was looking for a certain *someone*—for his darkest urge of all still awaited its performance.

With the arrival of autumn, the heat of Marrakesh became slightly less oppressive, inspiring Dorian to join up with some fellow foreigners on a caravan. His search had been fruitless; perhaps it would benefit him to leave the city for a while, thereby pausing from his quest to refresh himself. The event was being arranged by an elderly couple from Brighton by the name of Darlington whom he'd met entirely by chance one morning in the souk. Dorian's casual dispensing of advice to the lady regarding the excessive price of an enameled bracelet first led to dinner, then tea accompanied by shisha. Hearing he had spent time in Paris, a lively conversation about Surrealist art ensued, of which Dorian was fairly knowledgeable thanks to his association with some of the city's Surrealist artists (most notably the odd little fellow with the mustache). By the close of the evening Dorian had astonished himself by agreeing to accompany them on the caravan.

"We absolutely refuse to take no for an answer!" proclaimed Mrs. Darlington. Her thin wrist displayed the bracelet from the souk; she waved it dismissively in the air, as if the gesture settled the matter. "It will be the adventure of a lifetime!"

"Indeed!" rejoined Mr. Darlington, his face turning an alarming lobster-red from inhaling too much of the flavored tobacco. "We've wanted to do this for years—and I suspect we don't have very many remaining! Who knows, this might be our last adventure and they'll be bringing us back in wooden boxes!"

"Now I'm sure our young friend here doesn't wish to hear such morbid talk," scolded his wife with affection. "It will require more than a couple of camels to kill us off!"

Dorian found himself enjoying their company. The couple appeared harmless and even quite amusing in a quaint sort of way. He imagined he would be safe from discovery, the Darlingtons having made no mention of any names he recognized. It should be a diverting adventure, if nothing else. Although he questioned the wisdom of their embarking upon such an expedition at their advanced age, it was not his business to interfere. The travelers would be given an experienced guide along with several servants to take them by camel into the desert, where they were to set up tents for four consecutive nights—which to Dorian was more than sufficient when it came to forgoing his creature comforts. By the time they were set to embark, their ranks had doubled;

several more servants and an additional guide had to be recruited at the last minute.

With the group dressed from head to toe in Moroccan garb, it often proved difficult to determine everyone's identity as they journeyed forth into the desert. On several occasions Dorian lost his friends in the meandering line of camels and discovered himself resuming a line of conversation with people who had no notion what he was talking about. At one point he fell behind the others, using the lull to reflect upon the incredible vastness of the Sahara and the insignificance of his fellow adventurers, who were little more than specks of sand in this endless landscape. After a while the camel ahead of him also began to drop back, as if its rider desired to join Dorian's party of one.

"I say!" called the male voice belonging to the rider. "Are you all right back there?" The fellow spoke with an upper-class English accent. Dorian envisioned an Eton collar and school tie hiding beneath the flowing garments he'd adopted for the journey.

Squinting against the bright sunlight, Dorian signaled with a hand that he was perfectly well. This, however, did not appease the gentleman. Rather than resuming his previous pace, he shouted for the small brown fellow leading his camel to halt. Pushing back the hood of his djellaba in annoyance, he dug his fingers into what little remained of his hair as if the spartan white wisps had become infested with fleas. "Blasted sand!" he grumbled. "It gets everywhere! I daresay there won't be any bathtubs in our tents tonight, hey?"

Dorian's heart pitched sideways. Had he not tightened his hold on the reins, he would have tumbled off the back of his camel. The creature craned its long neck backward to hiss angrily at him, spraying him with foul-smelling spittle. Dorian blinked against the blinding light, hoping that what he saw before him was a mirage or hallucination brought on by the relentless sun and the monotony of the landscape. He had heard of such things happening to people in the desert. But when the man spoke again, he realized that what he saw was no trick of the eye.

Lord Gerald Oadby balanced precariously on the back of his camel, swearing under his breath as he continued to swat angrily at his scalp. Although the aging of his features made him nearly unrecognizable from the man Dorian had known in London, he knew the man's identity instantly from the glimpse he'd stolen in Paris, though now even less hair adorned his liver-spotted crown. Despite the tremor in Lord Gerald's voice, it had not altered as drastically as his physical appearance. Although the man was technically several years Dorian's senior, seeing him again reminded him of his own advanced age and the signs of decay he had thus far managed to evade.

Averting his face, Dorian pulled the hood of his garment forward, covering his golden-brown curls and well-shaped ears so that only his eyes, nose, and mouth could be seen. There seemed to be little else he could do to hide his identity, save for charging off into the desert on the back of his camel. Yet he was in the middle of the Sahara—in which direction would he go? Everything looked the same—rippling swathes of orange sand set beneath a torturous yellow sun. If it were possible for him to die, he could imagine doing so in this cruel landscape. By his estimation they had been riding for five hours. Could he retrace their trail back to the place from where they'd first set out? Hardly. What's more, he didn't have enough money in his pocket to pay the man leading his camel to take him there.

"Damn fool expedition, if you ask me," grumbled Lord Gerald. "One of my wife's harebrained schemes, no less." He indicated with his reins the camel up ahead of him which, Dorian concluded, transported the wide backside belonging to Lady Priscilla Oadby. The old man shook his head. "Bloody silly woman!" Reaching into a hidden pocket, he removed a wilted kerchief to mop the moisture from his flushed face, sighing with exasperation. "Dreadful place," he said. "Not fit for human habitation."

Dorian wondered how he would survive these next few days in the desert with the Oadbys at his side. He couldn't very well hide in his tent; indeed, they wouldn't even be set up until the evening, after the long day's ride had been completed. There was nothing for him to do but continue with this exercise in misery. In the meantime he'd keep as much of his face hidden as possible beneath the hood of his djellaba until he retired for the night. Perhaps he could claim that he had suffered from a bad burn after his exposure to the sun and wished not to inflict his unsightly visage on others. With any luck, the reports of the desert being freezing cold at night were true and everyone else would follow suit, thus sparing him from an explanation.

By now Lady Priscilla had managed to advance up the line of camel riders until she was equidistant from those at the front and Dorian and her husband at the rear. "Blasted woman thinks she's in a race!" muttered Lord Gerald, clearly irritated by his wife's progress. He called out to her several times, waving his arms in the air to attract her attention and nearly tipping off his camel before his camel-puller intervened in time. If the woman heard him, she gave no indication of it.

"I must catch up with my friends," said Dorian. He barked out a command in Berber to his camel-puller. With relief he found himself being led away from the still-grumbling Lord Oadby, whose stiffened posture indicated that he was quite miffed at being left on his own.

Avoiding the Oadbys for the duration of the expedition took away any enjoyment Dorian might have had in the experience. During the day he attached himself to the Darlingtons' side, wearing his hood so low over his brow that half the time he couldn't see where he was going. In the evenings he took to his tent with claims of feeling unwell, not even venturing out to dine with his fellow travelers, despite the savory aromas of lamb roasting on the spit. "Too much desert sun," he explained to anyone who enquired after his health. Thankfully his old friends from London were not among the concerned parties, though this did not embolden him to let down his guard. On the contrary, he kept the hood of his djellaba pulled low over his head at all times, even while eating food brought in to him by a servant.

When the desert explorers finally returned to Marrakesh, Dorian quit the party without so much as a good-bye, hastening back to the safety of his little house to wash away the fleas and sweat from his hair and body. The relief he felt at being home was such that he never wanted to venture out again. But as he stood naked before the mirror, perfuming his clean flesh with exotic oils, the burning need returned to him. Although he'd been granted a reprieve in the desert, it now reasserted itself with greater force, leaving the taste of ash on his tongue. He found his eyes roaming with the intense hunger of a lover the perfect contours of his form, stopping when they reached the flesh that rose upward from his loins. He took it into his hand, knowing that he could no longer wait for what he needed most.

Omar.

The name was music of the desert rich with all its cruelty and beauty. He was Dorian's physical opposite—dark while he was fair, coarse while he was refined, his eyes two burning coals promising a passion that had more to do with violence than any form of love. Omar was just another impoverished boy-man trying to survive by eking out a disreputable living in the alleyways of Marrakesh—and Dorian would be the one who provided it.

Like his benefactor, Omar's appearance of youth was highly deceptive. Youth is often equated with inexperience and purity, and to see him from a distance one might easily mistake Omar for possessing these qualities. Other qualities, such as cruelty and brutality could only be detected on closer view, for they manifested themselves at the mouth and in the eyes. Coming face to face with Omar for the first time, Dorian saw them in all their ruthless glory.

He had finally found what he'd been searching for.

Dorian was astonished that the young man had told him his name and more astonished that he had asked for it. The squalid encounters he sought in the alleyways of the medina did not include such things as polite introductions. Nevertheless, one had been forthcoming, and it had been made in English. "I am Omar," was all he'd said before taking Dorian against a wall in the alleyway without even the benefit of spitting into his palm to prepare for entry. It was the act of an animal, but with a crudeness that only a human could be capable of. The very baseness of it suggested a rage spawned by deprivation and envy and perhaps a denial of one's true nature. Dorian had seen this denial before in men who refused to acknowledge that their passions were for others of their sex.

Indeed, Omar was everything he'd dreamed of. He had chosen well.

The young man's guttural grunting belied any possibility for discretion in this public setting; even the sightless would have been able to discern the nature of what was transpiring. The fact that several of his companions, many of whom Dorian had serviced on his knees on previous nights, leaned casually against the opposite wall taking in the proceedings made the shame taste all the more delicious on his tongue—like sweet golden honey mixed with something sharp and tart.

Dorian dropped down onto the cobblestones in an exaggerated crouch so that Omar could fill him fully and without hindrance. He felt like a circus animal under the power of a harsh master, though he welcomed all that was done to him. The burning sting of each thrust was as excruciating as a chili pepper being rubbed into an open wound and as exquisite as the touch of fine silk against the fingertips. Dorian experienced the added humiliation of tears as they coursed freely down his cheeks, his chest rocking with quiet sobs. Rather than pulling away, he swallowed each cry of pain. Indeed, how his body had been hungering for this moment!

He could feel the young man's rage vibrating through

his prick, the tip of which was like a fat lump of burning coal as it forced its way deeper until it seemed as if it would sear his internal organs. As if desiring to inflict further havoc upon his victim, Omar shimmied his pelvis from side and side, stretching Dorian wide until he feared he'd be left torn and bleeding and quite likely robbed of his money and even his clothing when it was all over. Yet he knew it would be worth it as he experienced a pleasure unlike any he'd ever imagined as Omar robbed him in other ways, stealing his dignity and his control, only to commit the ultimate indignity by ejaculating inside him. It went on forever, as if a pipe had burst, flooding Dorian's interior until it seemed that even his belly had begun to swell. When he felt his own release erupting from him in response, his degradation was complete.

Omar withdrew as roughly as he'd first entered, leaving Dorian crouched on the filthy cobblestones, his naked posterior with its battered opening in plain view. Suddenly he felt something warm and wet land in the cleft of his buttocks as Omar hawked, then spat. It was followed by the sound of footfalls moving away as he went to rejoin his friends who had reassembled beneath the archway, where they awaited the next customer desperate for male flesh.

Tears continued to fall down Dorian's cheeks, but now they were tears of enlightenment. He had transcended some spiritual plane he had never anticipated. What had transpired tonight was a masterpiece of art that surpassed anything his old friend Basil Hallward or his Surrealist companions in Paris could have given birth to with paint. He wanted to remain like this all through the night and into the brightness of morning, on display for the whole world to see and admire. Dorian's chest swelled with pride as he imagined how beautiful he must look in his defilement; he yearned for a second pair of eyes so that he could see himself as he now was. Such exalted moments were rare, even in a lifetime as prolonged as his. He could feel himself growing hard all over again as he reflected upon the sordidness of his condition. He took his erection into his hand, working toward a swift climax, the results joining the froth that still glistened against the dark cobblestones.

The sound of approaching male voices speaking in Darija Arabic eventually returned him to his senses. He was naked from the waist down in a poor part of the medina; many here would find neither beauty nor exultation in his exhibition. Hauling his trousers up from his ankles, he rose to standing, rubbing the muck that had been ground into his hands onto his garments. A bead of blood had formed on the heel of his palm and when he glanced down, he noticed that one of the knees on his trousers had several spots of blood staining the white cloth. It was then that he noticed the shards of glass scattered like dirty chips of ice on the cobbles. He hadn't even felt the injuries.

There was no sign of Omar or any of his companions beneath the archway or anywhere in the twisting alleyway. There was also no sign of the roll of francs Dorian had kept in the pocket of his gandora. The money he cared not a fig for. Of that he had plenty; indeed, he would have been happy to part with a substantial amount of his fortune to experience such pleasures again. He couldn't remember ever feeling so alive. Suddenly Lord Henry's face appeared before him, his expression salaciously approving. He'd told Dorian to live for the senses and had practiced it himself. But would dear Harry have done tonight what Dorian had had the courage to do?

Some weeks went by before he saw Omar again. Each night that brought disappointment was another night of anguish as Dorian walked up and down the same shabby alleyway, willing the young man to be there, perhaps awaiting the return of his English benefactor. He knew how desperate he must have looked to the others gathered there waiting for other men like himself. He could hear them laughing about the "lovesick *pédéraste*" as he passed. "Omar is busy fucking a Spaniard!" they'd taunt as they lounged beneath the archway smoking their strong Turkish cigarettes. The one who had kicked Dorian in the belly would pull out his prick and wave it at him like a dog wagging its tail, calling out: "I let you suck for free!"

Despite their laughter and jeers, Dorian continued to visit the alleyway, determined to locate Omar at all costs, some secret part of him taking pleasure in the humiliation of being the "lovesick *pédéraste*." Perhaps it was true, for he couldn't get Omar out of his mind. He had become obsessed with the swarthy boy-man with the fury in his heart. The thought of Omar being with a Spaniard—or anyone else for that matter—was something he couldn't bear to think about. Although the evidence told him that Omar loitered in the alleyway to sell his sexual favors to men, some innate sense of possessiveness made Dorian hope it was not so, that it had been Fate which led them both to the same alleyway on the same night. Perhaps this might explain why he had not seen Omar here again.

Fidelity was not a concept to which Dorian gave

much credence. Anything that restricted one's desire for pleasure and sensation was, in his view, the ultimate of evils; therefore he was puzzled that he didn't want Omar to bestow his violent passions upon another. He wanted them all for himself. He had money enough to buy their exclusivity and this Dorian was determined to do, provided he could locate the young man whose black eyes burned with untold—and perhaps as yet *unrealized*—cruelties.

And then one night Omar was there beneath the archway. *Waiting.*

Dorian moved Omar into his little walled-in house in the medina, where he saw to it that all his needs were met and more—such luxuries as he could provide not being something the young man had ever been accustomed to. Omar was fed and clothed and encouraged to avail himself of the poppy, of which Dorian kept a continuous supply. He went to great lengths in his generosity, though his reasons had little to do with any sudden benevolence of the heart: Dorian wished to limit any necessity for his guest to leave the house. He dared not risk Omar falling back into his old habits, which he feared might happen should he reestablish contact with his associates from the alleyway. Not that Dorian had much reason for concern. As he came to spend more time in the young man's company, he discovered that Omar was of an indolent nature and generally disinclined toward the pursuit of a living, even if such a living required nothing more than the occasional employment of his prick. Dorian likewise discovered that his guest was not the most social of animals. On the contrary, Omar possessed a sullen and unpleasant disposition and had little to say except to demand something from his benefactor. His manners were coarse at best and his language foul and abusive, even when he was in a good humor. Such displeasing personality traits were of no consequence. Dorian hadn't brought Omar into his life for intellectual discourse or to accompany him to social functions.

Although the dynamics of the relationship never altered, Omar had become a kind of concubine—but his role was not passive. He remained the aggressor and, at least on the surface, exerted total control over Dorian. In reality, Dorian was the puppet master pulling the strings; nothing that transpired between them happened without his full and eager compliance. Since Dorian was still in the heat of the relationship, it was difficult to foresee a time when he would grow weary of his companion, yet he knew it was inevitable, as with any close interaction between human beings. Therefore their relationship was not exclusive—at least not on Dorian's side. As Lord Henry had once told him: "The only horrible thing in the world is ennui, Dorian. That is the one sin for which there is no forgiveness."

While Omar remained at home passing his hours in an opium-induced fugue, Dorian pursued whatever means of pleasure were available to him. He was discovering a new dimension to the city that did not include squalid alleyways, meeting foreigners like himself who were as keen to explore their darker sides as he was—and as keen to share their exploits. They assembled in various homes and private clubs throughout Marrakesh to exchange stories of their conquests, taking vicarious gratification from the luridness of the tales being told and assuaging their needs with any number of partners present. With his youth and exquisite beauty, Dorian quickly became the star player in these social events. Despite his unwillingness to make the nature of his relationship with Omar public by being seen in his company, he was not in the least reluctant to share with his new companions every intimate detail of what transpired between them, particularly those details relating to his degradation. His candor astonished even him, yet there was another reason for confessing to his newfound love of personal defilement—it gave him tremendous pleasure to do so. Revealing the particulars to his audience meant reliving these moments all over again. Indeed, the taste of his shame proved so much sweeter when shared.

Although many of the gentlemen were visibly excited by Dorian's revelations, the ladies appeared the most affected. They gathered around Dorian like adoring worshippers, seating themselves at his feet as he held court with his latest tale of debasement. Several members of his female audience began to indulge in self-pleasure, and even a number of men took themselves in hand for the same purpose. The more they shouted out their protests of "Shocking!" and "We cannot bear to hear any more!" the swifter the fingers of the ladies moved between their thighs and the swifter the hands of the gentlemen moved at their laps until the room exploded with the sounds and scents of pleasure.

It had been some time since Dorian had enjoyed the bodies of women and he decided to amuse himself with his new companions, finding their yielding flesh and girlish giggles a refreshing change from the relentless hardness of men. There was also an even more important purpose for his renewed interest—he knew the effect it would have on Omar, whose poppy habit had increased to alarming levels in recent weeks, undoubtedly due to having nothing to occupy his time other than brutalizing Dorian until his approach had become merely routine.

Lord Henry's comment about the sin of ennui had been playing inside Dorian's mind like a recording on a phonograph whose needle was stuck in a groove. He believed Omar was losing his edge and becoming too complacent. Perhaps he only had himself to blame, for the idle young man had nothing to prove and no impetus to go out of his way to earn his keep, which was already being provided to him. If he hoped to maintain the freshness and excitement for a while longer, he needed to adopt a new strategy in his dealings with Omar.

It had never required much to set the young man off on a violent tangent. Therefore Dorian, wishing to encourage and exacerbate such episodes, would return home before dawn after being with any number of women, their combined scents marking him like a cat marks its territory. He'd find Omar waiting for him like a jealous husband, his fingers curled into tight fists, his eyes burning with the black fires of fury. He looked like a man standing on the threshold of murder. "Where have you been?" he'd bellow, fighting off the slothful effects of his favorite pastime. Dorian was amazed that he still had the ability to function, particularly in the bedroom. Men twice his size would have been comatose. But not Omar.

No sooner did Dorian enter the house than he began to taunt his lover with the specifics of how he'd passed his time, sparing no detail, regardless of how repugnant the recipient found it. Cursed and condemned with every foul epitaph known to man, Dorian crouched on the cold floor tiles like a frightened rabbit as Omar tore into him from behind, sobbing with the force of his rage. Just as Dorian believed he'd experienced the best his lover had to offer, he would be presented with still further brutality that left him stunned and bleeding and filled with reverence. That he should require the attention of a physician on several occasions was a disadvantage Dorian was prepared to accept as part of the benefits of living a life that demanded extreme sensations. Had he known then that the generous bestowal of francs he'd deposited on the practitioner's examination table each time he sought his services would add fuel to the rumors already circulating about him in Marrakesh he might have decided to tolerate his injuries rather than seek their remedy from a fellow Englishman in possession of a loose tongue. But oh, the exquisite joys that had led him there!

There was scarcely an hour of the day when Omar could not be seen with the pipe. His dependence on the poppy had by this time become engraved upon him, his once-prepossessing visage tarnished by the telltale smudges of soot beneath the eyes, his lips turning the shade of raw liver. As his jet-black hair became scattered with ashy gray and his smooth flesh took on the quality of worn leather, Dorian heard the tolling of a familiar bell in his mind's ear. If he'd only heeded the warning instead of lingering in Marrakesh, matters might have turned out very differently indeed.

Omar's deterioration continued at a steady pace, owing not only to his addiction but also to the passing of time. It was inevitable that the enduring youth and beauty of his English lover would pain Omar like a crown of thorns upon his head. Like Madame Cherie before him, he put the question to Dorian, only in a less playful tone. In fact, his words were sharp and accusatory, as if his benefactor had found a way to steal his years and claim them for himself. Such an idea was hardly preposterous to someone deficient in education and abundant in superstition. No matter how many times Dorian tried to make this aging boy recognize the absurdity of his argument, Omar refused to be satisfied. "You have tricked me!" he'd cry, his voice tormented by despair. "You are sucking the life from my bones!"

Unable to supply an answer for Omar or even for himself, Dorian would simply walk away, hoping such unpleasantries would pass as quickly as they'd appeared. He had no explanation to offer other than the tragic reality that Omar was growing old, as nature intended, while Dorian continued to retain the appearance of one barely out of boyhood. There was nothing he could say to appease him or take away his pain—and Dorian had no desire to do the latter, since it heightened the rages.

Omar became obsessed with the juxtaposition of his decay against the youthful countenance of his lover, who looked as young and fresh as the day they'd first met under the archway in the squalid alleyway. He remained convinced there was some form of witchery at work and considered even the most mundane household trinket suspect in the casting of a spell. Although Dorian recognized that some form of godless witchery was, in fact, responsible for his condition, he dared not speak of his suspicions to Omar. He hadn't even spoken of it to Lord Henry. Over the years he reflected on it less and less, choosing instead to enjoy the sweet fruits of this curious gift, regardless of whether they'd been delivered to him on the Devil's pitchfork.

But Omar would not remain silent about his suspicions. He had begun to speak out of turn to others. No longer was he content to simply remain in the house having his every need and whim catered to. Instead he demanded that Dorian take him to bars and cafés and even out shopping in the souk, where he insisted on being fitted for the tailored Western garments Dorian had come to shun, only to neglect them after their construction had been completed. It was as if he wished to deliberately draw attention to himself, neither realizing nor caring that his physical appeal had long since waned. The only thing that hadn't waned was his brutality—which was the only reason Dorian had kept him around for so long.

Whenever they were together in public Omar linked his arm with Dorian's, walking with a decidedly girlish gait that drew dark looks from many of the locals. Dorian's heart leapt with dread, for there had been rumors of stonings taking place in the poorer sections of the city—mostly of well-heeled foreign gentlemen accused of corrupting the minds and bodies of young men and boys. The young girls who'd fallen victim to similar circumstances were also stoned to death—usually by fathers and brothers desperate to cast off the veil of shame that resulted from their daughters and sisters' "actions." Dorian had no wish to test his mortality by joining their ranks.

Omar had to be removed from the equation.

Considering the circumstances of his existence, it was inevitable the relationship would end; Dorian was merely hastening the time of its demise. There would be other Omars in other lands with whom he could enjoy similar adventures—the loss of one would prey on his mind but a moment.

Opportunity presented itself in the pre-dawn hours of a Friday when Dorian returned home after a night of indulgence, the scent of women still pungent on his body. This being a holy day, none of the servants were expected. Although he paid them generously to ensure their silence regarding the aging opium addict with whom Dorian shared his house, he thought it best to take no chances for what he had in mind.

Omar had started on the pipe long before sundown. His eyes possessed their usual sloth when they turned toward Dorian, who seated himself on the adjacent cushion, indicating that he wished to partake. Omar's nostrils quivered in distaste and he pulled the pipe out of reach. "You have been with whores again!" he shouted, his eyes burning with dark fury.

A slow smile spread across Dorian's lips, which had been made all the rosier from spending a good portion of the evening between the thighs of his female companions. "*Whores?* I assure you, my darling Omar, no money ever exchanged hands."

Omar spat on the floor—a rather filthy habit of which Dorian had been unsuccessful in breaking him. "Hah! A whore is still a whore—and *all* women are whores!"

Dorian's smile turned to one of indulgence, as if he were humoring an ill-tempered child. He was well aware that this always had the effect of intensifying Omar's rages, which was precisely why he did it. "I beg to differ," he said. "One of the ladies whose companionship I enjoyed this evening was a marquess—and a very agreeable one at that!" Bringing his middle finger up to his lips, Dorian licked it with relish, watching bloody murder flash in Omar's eyes. He felt a stirring in his trousers; it intensified into a full-scale erection with Omar's next words.

"I should kill you."

Dorian began to laugh. "But then who would you fuck with such divine brutality? You yourself told me that no man alive would be able to bear it, let alone allow another of his sex to perform such a filthy act upon him. Have you not said so many times? Do you not condemn me, dear Omar, for being your…" and here Dorian paused dramatically, "*whore*?"

Omar frowned thoughtfully, silently acquiescing that what Dorian had said was in all probability true, though this didn't lessen his disgust toward his philandering lover. Suddenly he looked directly into Dorian's eyes. "Maybe I should fuck you right now—fuck you until the blood spurts from that devil's hole of yours like the neck of a slaughtered sheep. I'll enjoy watching that after I've planted my seed in you."

Dorian felt his prick judder violently; it was nearly in danger of spilling its release. He was getting Omar exactly where he wanted him—enraged and merciless and, as he discovered when he reached into his lap, rock hard.

"You have cursed me"—sobbed Omar—"cursed me with your filth!"

Dorian held out a finger to Omar's lips—the same one he'd licked. "Would you like to have a taste? I assure you it is most delightful."

The blow to his head came as a surprise. Omar lashed out, hitting him with the ceramic pipe. A trickle of blood burned Dorian's left eye from the cut now etched into his smooth forehead. That his beauty remained unmarred gouged a hole in Omar's heart that filled quickly with poison, intensifying his wrath and his hatred for this highborn Englishman whose physical perfection never waned, no matter how many years went past.

Flipping him over as if he weighed no more than a child's rag doll, Omar tore the trousers from Dorian's hips, exposing his pale buttocks to the cool air. Dorian found his bloodied forehead being ground into the floor tiles as a pair of strong hands pulled him open. "I will make you pay!" cried a tortured voice behind him. Still dazed from the blow to his head, it took a moment before he realized that the voice belonged to Omar. Dorian felt a globule of saliva make a perfect landing and felt another judder of anticipation vibrate through his erect flesh. Could his life possibly be any more exquisite?

Omar battered Dorian mercilessly from behind, each stroke a dull blade stabbing into him and prompting his eyes to overflow with tears. It was nearly as perfect as their first encounter in the alleyway but for the fact there was no audience to witness his disgrace. Omar condemned his lover as if he were a creature sent from Hell to torment him, his every movement designed to inflict the utmost pain and distress as if this might somehow exorcise the evil demon whose opening he was doomed to fill. His mule-like ignorance, his surety that he was causing harm when, in reality, he was feeding Dorian's passions, was the only thing that gave Dorian pause for what he needed to do next.

Suddenly Dorian felt Omar pulsating deep inside him as liquid fire burst forth into his abused passage. With one final curse, Omar withdrew, only to plunge his fist inside Dorian, whose climax arrived with such intensity that he broke down in sobs, sounding like a man whose spirit had been destroyed. He spent the best part of an hour curled up into a ball on the cold tiles, reliving the moments that had just passed and wondering if he would ever achieve such bliss again. The pleasure resulting from his pain had been worth it, yet he also felt sadness, since this would be the last pleasure he received from this once-youthful boy of the medina.

For tonight would be Omar's last night alive. A few more hours of the pipe until the appropriate stage of oblivion had been achieved, followed by a pillow over his nose and mouth took away the last breaths of Omar's life. All that remained was the rather unseemly disposal of his body—a circumstance upon which Dorian preferred not to reflect. It brought to mind the memory of Basil Hallward, all traces of whom had been dispatched with thanks to modern science and the art of blackmail.

Back then Dorian had been fortunate enough to have the talents of his old friend Alan Campbell at his disposal—a man of science who had harbored a secret he would have given anything to prevent being exposed. The application of nitric acid had eliminated all evidence of Hallward's existence, though it had not come without a price. For Campbell the price would eventually be his suicide. For Dorian it was the further deterioration of his portrait, which next showed the subject's hands glistening with blood, some of which oozed from the canvas.

As for the subject's face, it had become a thing of such unspeakable horror that merely to look upon it would drive a man to madness. Indeed, perhaps it had already done so.

* * *

An anxiously hovering waiter returned Dorian to the present and the now-tepid glass of tea on the table. He wondered how long it had been there. His fugue left in its wake a jumble of images as disconcerting as they were pleasing. Perhaps this was what came from having lived as long as he had. He could not recall the last time he'd taken a sip of the tea. That was when he noticed a dead fly floating in the glass among a few errant tea leaves. Pushing it away in disgust, Dorian ordered another, willing his mind back to lucidity. He was so grateful when the freshly brewed glass of tea arrived that he burned his tongue in his haste to drink. The surge of sugar seemed to wedge his brain back into place and return him to familiarity. He was at his favorite café. The call to prayer had ended and everyone was going about their normal activities, including the waiter, who was weaving his way through the tables carrying his hammered tray loaded with glasses of tea and plates of sticky pastries.

The café had filled up since Dorian first arrived, and he regretted not having ordered one of the pastries. As he turned to signal the waiter, he noticed the elderly couple seated a few tables away who'd been observing him earlier. They were now speaking covertly to each other and staring pointedly in his direction, not bothering to conceal their interest. The pair rose up from their chairs and began to move in his direction. The gentleman relied on a walking stick, stopping every few moments to support his weight upon it and use the interlude to speak in an excited tone to his female companion. Eventually they reached Dorian's table, which appeared to be their intended destination.

The sweetness of Dorian's tea suddenly turned sour on his tongue.

The old woman's crinkled features shifted themselves into an expression of astonishment. "As I live and breathe!" she cried, looking as if living and breathing were not activities she or her companion would be engaging in for much longer. "Gerald, it cannot be possible that this is our old friend from London!"

The aged gentleman leaned heavily on his walking stick, his lips opening and closing like a fish gulping its last breath. "I say, is that you, Dorian?" he finally managed to gasp.

"Surely this cannot be our Dorian Gray!" chimed his companion. "And after all these years!" A strange light appeared in her rheumy eyes as they took in Dorian from the golden-brown tendrils of hair that fell over his smooth brow to the leather tips of the babouches on his feet. "And gone native, I see."

"Indeed, my dear, did I not say as much to you in Paris? Did I not say that I had seen our Dorian Gray in the flesh with my very own eyes? Ah—but you would not believe me!" The old man gave forth a wheezing laugh that sounded as though it had originated from the bottom of a dried-up well. "And you told me what a fool I was to write to Lord Henry with the news!"

Time had not been kind to either of the Oadbys. Dorian hadn't encountered the couple since the long-ago desert expedition that had sent him into hiding, yet he could see how drastically the years and their dissolute lifestyles had altered their appearances. That this could be the same man Dorian had allowed to pleasure him by mouth, or this the same woman they had both shared, was beyond comprehension. Trying to suppress a shudder, he steeled himself for his reply, hoping they wouldn't prove difficult. Surely they would realize that the limitations of human biology made it impossible for him to be the young man from their past. "Begging your pardon, but I fear you have mistaken me for someone else," he said, regarding them with an indifferent smile.

The old man grinned, displaying rotting teeth that caused another shudder to pass through Dorian. "My dear fellow, if you are *not* Dorian Gray, then you're the reincarnation of him!"

"That voice! Why, I should know it anywhere! It is music to the ear!" Lady Priscilla leaned in close to Dorian until their noses were nearly touching, the sickly-sweet smell of perfume and decaying flesh choking him. "But we thought you were dead! The fire—"

"Does he look dead to you?" rejoined her husband. He presented Dorian with a meaningful leer, his gray tongue licking hungrily over his lips with the memory of what it had once tasted. "Anything *but*, I'd say."

Dorian felt a flush staining his pale cheeks as he pulled back from Lady Oadby's advance. The couple's rapacious stares intensified until he felt as if they had invaded his body with their fingers. Both looked as if they wished to consume every inch of him and would have done so were they not in a public place. "Perhaps I must be a doppelganger for this Dorian Gray fellow of yours, dead or otherwise," he replied with a humor that failed to thaw the blue ice in his eyes.

Lord Gerald looked at Dorian like a schoolmaster who had just caught his pupil in a lie. "I know it to be impossible, my dear fellow, but how did you manage it? You don't look a day older than when we last saw you.

And that was…" he paused, glancing toward his wife for confirmation. "How many years has it been?"

"Why, forty, at least!" offered Lady Priscilla, her eyes aglow with the same memories that gave Dorian's sensibilities such pain. "And what delightful times we shared!" Without waiting to be invited, she settled herself in the vacant chair across from Dorian while her husband leaned unsteadily on his walking stick, looking ready to collapse in a heap to the ground. Suddenly she grabbed Dorian's hand, which had been resting innocently on the table. "Do you remember how you and Gerald used to fill me at both ends? Why, it was as though I'd died and gone to heaven!"

"Yes! It took a bit of doing, but by Jingo, we finally managed it!" chirruped her husband. "I've always found that a bit of lard can go a long way in these cases."

"Be that as it may," interrupted his wife, "there's nothing quite so efficiently greased as an excited woman!"

"Point taken, my dear."

Dorian felt his gorge rising. Indeed, the couple appeared to be quite mad! Finishing the now-cold dregs of his tea, he performed the requisite movements of a man readying to depart on matters more pressing than idle chatter. Reclaiming his hand from Lady Priscilla's claw-like grip, he pushed back his chair with a loud scrape on the pavement and stood up. "I do hope you find this friend of yours. I bid you good day." With a polite incline of his head, he left the table, his empty glass a poignant reminder of the pleasant afternoon he'd been passing before his past had caught up with him.

Rather than heading directly home, Dorian decided to go in a random direction, should the Oadbys be of a mind to follow. He had no wish for them to discover where he lived—or, for that matter, where he spent his leisure time. It was bothersome enough that they'd happened upon his café. In a world turned on its head from the moment Basil Hallward's brush had painted Dorian's image on canvas, any small moment of routine had become as rare as a pearl shat from a goose's backside—and as valuable. He would either need to find a more out-of-the-way café in which to partake of his afternoon ritual or give it up entirely—or at least until such time as the Oadbys quit Marrakesh, providing they'd not taken up residence like so many other foreigners fleeing the ravages of war. The fact that he had not seen them since the desert caravan expedition all those years ago gave him hope that their purpose in the city was to visit rather than to occupy a permanent home.

Despite these repeated self-assurances that the couple's stay was only of a temporary nature, Dorian was plagued with bouts of sleeplessness that not even the divine poppy could remedy. For educated people such as Lord and Lady Oadby to believe that the young Dorian Gray of their past was now a man of greatly advanced years whose appearance hadn't altered since the late nineteenth century? Surely they must have realized their folly and forgotten all about him!

But they had not. Like the effluvium from a pile of dung, the Oadbys were everywhere, making their ponderous way up and down every winding street and alleyway, drinking tea in every café, passing outside the high walls of Dorian's house as he stood on the upstairs balcony smoking a cigarette in the breeze blowing in from the sea. He had even spied them in the souk, barely managing to conceal himself behind a stack of dusty rugs before they saw him. No matter where he went, the couple was there or not far behind, as tenacious and unpleasant as a bad tooth. Even his favorite opium den, which had always been the source of much ease and relaxation, had become a place to avoid. They appeared to be pursuing him from one end of Marrakesh to another, as were various colorful reports of his activities. Unbeknownst to Dorian, Lord and Lady Oadby were closely associated with the English physician who'd treated him for the rather distinctive malady caused by his activities with Omar. Such reports were given additional hue by those who had spied Dorian out in public with his male lover, whose recent disappearance had not gone unnoticed. The nature of their relationship was no longer much of a secret to anyone; Dorian's determination to blend in with the locals had begun to unravel the moment he'd set foot in the physician's office.

Dorian had become a hunted animal. He hadn't experienced anything like this since Sibyl Vane's vengeful brother James had hounded him in London after realizing that Dorian was the "Prince Charming" of whom his dead sister had spoken with such love. Were it not for a fortuitous hunting accident, James Vane wouldn't have rested until he'd seen the man who had been the cause of his sister's suicide dead.

What did the Oadbys want? Did they wish to blackmail him or were they deranged enough to believe they could resume their previous dalliances?

Casting his mind back, Dorian recalled a certain possessiveness in their natures that set his hackles on end. For the most part he'd ignored it, but it was returning to him like drops of water forming a puddle. Rather than accepting that he had free will to indulge himself with whomever he pleased and with as many partners as he pleased, Lord Gerald and Lady Priscilla had turned greedy and clinging, deciding they wanted Dorian all to themselves. The fact that the couple had freely indulged with any number of men and women made their demands on him a study in hypocrisy. However, all this had changed as they began to turn away from the companionship of others save for their favorite companion of all.

Suddenly the Oadbys were nowhere to be seen, choosing to stay sequestered inside their grand home in Mayfair rather than attend any functions that presented the opportunity of physical dalliances with their hedonistic contemporaries. Most assumed they had at last grown weary of the endless variety of flesh on offer; Dorian knew otherwise. Having enjoyed their companionship, he continued to visit them, indulging in any number of activities that two men and one woman could conceive of. His encounters with the Oadbys eventually became tarnished by tedium, although in this instance it was hastened by the pair's dogged persistence that Dorian remove himself from the society of others and take up permanent residence in their home. The suggestion eventually took on the tone of a demand; they refused to accept his unwillingness to be exclusive to them. They even engaged the services of a jeweler in Clerkenwell to fashion a gold ring engraved with their names for Dorian to wear around the base of his prick. Although he'd accepted the gift, he never wore it. When they later recommended he have their names inked across the flawless contours of his chest like a brand, he severed all ties. It was clear the couple desired to own him.

And it was clear they desired to do so again, many decades later.

He wasn't going to be rid of them unless he took some form of action. It wasn't difficult to locate unsavory individuals in Marrakesh willing to do most anything for a few francs; Dorian had learned this firsthand when he required assistance in dispensing with Omar. With war raging in several countries, there were even more dubious characters populating the city. However, he preferred to leave this option as a last resort. His biggest concern was that they'd already spoken to others about his presence in Marrakesh, which could place him in the spotlight should something untoward happen to the couple. Perhaps they might leave the city and go elsewhere, in which case he had nothing to worry about. He just needed to be patient.

Dorian decided to significantly reduce the amount of time he spent out on the streets. Cafés and the souk were now off limits, as were most locations of a public nature. He only went out after dark—and even this was undertaken with discretion. His physical needs warred constantly with the necessity to remain out of view; he found himself longing to revisit the alleyway in which he'd met Omar. It seemed doubtful that the same men still loitered under the archway, having become too seasoned for those seeking the illicit services of fresh young males. Yet he dared not go near the place, fearing more than anything that he would meet with Omar's angry ghost seeking to avenge his murder.

Fortunately there was one place remaining in the city on which he could rely for sanctuary. Dorian had been there a handful of times over the years, finding it an amusing place to spend the dark hours leading up to dawn. The quality of the poppy was excellent, as was the quality of pleasure companion, should one be sufficiently *compos mentis* to partake. The establishment was operated by an old Chinese woman known as Mrs. Chang, though it remained to be seen whether this was her true name; the war had filled the city with many who were not what they claimed.

A tiny but intimidating creature, Mrs. Chang liked no one, especially foreign gentlemen with pale flesh who spoke the King's English. Dorian was one of the few she allowed through her door, for even *she* could not resist the roses of his lips or the guileless blue of his eyes, though this did not earn him a smile. Indeed, the woman seemed physically incapable of such an undertaking. Her visage was fixed in a perpetual scowl of mistrust, her every word emerging as a hostile bark that did a superior job of keeping Dorian's fellow Englishmen away.

In these rooms, veiled in a permanent blue curtain of smoke, the evenings blended into night and eventually into dawn, at which time Dorian wound his way back to his little home in the medina to sleep away the heat of the day before returning to Mrs. Chang's at nightfall. The routine proved so pleasing that he soon forgot all about the loss of his glass of tea in the afternoons, the memory of it fading along with the recent presences of Lord and Lady Oadby. He felt cocooned in a protective cloud where nothing could harm him. Life had become simple and uncomplicated again. Although no stranger to the fragrant plant, Dorian began to understand the appeal it had held for his former lover, who'd been unable to pass more than a few hours without it. He enjoyed the slowing down of his senses, followed by the delicious lethargy of his limbs as he reached for the nearest available body. It mattered not whether it were female or male, only that it was warm and willing to surrender to his needs.

Dorian partook of the pipe with impunity, trying to achieve an oblivion where the past could no longer haunt him. Unlike Omar, he would not develop dark circles beneath his eyes or a dependence that could not be broken. Nothing seemed capable of destroying him. For this he owed thanks to the portrait Basil Hallward had painted. It made sense that as long as the painting survived intact, so too would he. It had been a stroke of genius to secure it below ground in a concrete bunker. Not even Hitler's most valiant efforts would be capable of destroying it. Dorian dared not imagine what it looked like now.

To think that he had once taken such perverse pleasure in going upstairs to the little schoolroom to compare his perfect countenance to that of the decaying version in the portrait. Holding a mirror before his face, Dorian compared the virtuous image in the glass against the one his eyes viewed on the canvas, feeling himself hardening as the portrayal of his sins was revealed to him with ever more gruesome vibrancy. Seeing how he truly looked sent a breath of madness whispering into his ear, encouraging him to take his erection into his hand, caressing himself before the painting's leering blood-filled eyes until his fluids joined those that leeched from the canvas in clots of dripping gore. It was as if Dorian wished to mock the hideous image with the display of his beautifully formed manhood and the pleasure he derived from it as he gazed upon the ugliness before him. At times he would stand on a chair and press the bulb of his prick against the thing's corrupt lips, expecting them to open. The imagined sensation of his victory as he spent himself inside that fetid mouth was enough to make him climax in earnest, certain that he had finally lost his mind when a rotting tongue appeared to lick away his fluids.

Then Hettie Merton had come into his life, along with his final bid for redemption. Dorian had believed he'd fallen in love—a true and pure love that convinced him he still had a chance to live a life of goodness. Rather than tainting the innocent country girl with his venality, he had spared her, leaving her undisgraced. Indeed, by sacrificing his desires for the good of another, he expected the evils he had committed to drop from him like scales shed by a snake. How Lord Henry had ridiculed him when he reported to him his noble deed—the deed he expected would save him from eternal damnation.

His mentor's derision resounded as clearly in his ears as if it had taken place only yesterday. Dorian had been seated at the piano, playing a Chopin concerto until at last he could bear no more. He wanted to know what dear Harry would say if he knew that Dorian had murdered the allegedly missing Basil Hallward, whom everyone believed had vanished after arriving in Paris. Rather than being repulsed by the notion, Lord Henry had mocked Dorian still further by his disbelief that his friend could even be capable of committing such a deed. "Crime belongs exclusively to the lower orders," he had said. "I don't blame them in the smallest degree. I should fancy that crime was to them what art is to us, simply a method of procuring extraordinary sensations."

Dorian had been crushed. Not only did Lord Henry

dismiss the notion of him murdering someone, but he'd dismissed it by reason of social class! He knew then that he could never allow his friend to see his portrait. When questioned as to its whereabouts, he continued to assert that it had gone astray en route to his home in Selby, hoping this concluded the matter. The painting would remain his shameful secret until the very end—or until it reverted back to how it had looked on the afternoon Basil Hallward first presented it to them.

That his portrait would return to its formerly pristine state now that he had changed was, in Dorian's mind, an absolute certainty. He had owned his sins and was willing to live out the rest of his days in penitence for them. The evil on the canvas would fade away until the under-layer revealed the beautiful man whose youth and purity had been captured in paint. Yet later when he went to the old schoolroom to check on its progress, Dorian discovered it to be more loathsome than ever. The putrefying visage had twisted into a sneer that made him realize the absurdity of what he'd set out to do. His decision to live a life of goodness had been nothing but an act of hypocrisy driven by the desire to experience a new sensation. Finally understanding the full truth of what he'd become, Dorian had to destroy the only evidence remaining of his crimes: the portrait.

But to destroy it would have meant destroying himself—and this he could not do. His love of vice and of himself was far too great to allow human mortality to stand in his way.

Closing his eyes against the memory, Dorian took a long draught from the pipe, drawing the fragrant smoke deep into his lungs and chasing out the nightmare of his painted image. He harbored no regrets. He could no longer conceive of a life with restrictions or morals prescribed by some dusty tome of suspect authorship. The paradise it promised was one he'd already found.

Fingertips brushed against his arm as a hand reached out seeking the pipe. It belonged to his immediate neighbor—a petite young lady whose skin was like the blush of a peach. Dorian might have leaned over to kiss her had she not been busily engaged with pair of local gentlemen as dark as the Moroccan night. Both of them appeared to be sharing the same opening. The older fellow, whom Dorian was certain he recognized from the souk, lay like a bed beneath her while the younger crouched at her upended rump, forcing her legs back toward her shoulders until her knees framed her ears. The young lady appeared to be dealing with the matter quite capably and had even insinuated a hand between her thighs to add further stimulation to the proceedings.

Dorian was delighted that Mrs. Chang's dislike of foreigners didn't extend to the fairer sex. On the contrary, the establishment had a reputation for catering to foreign females with pale flesh and a lust for fruits that were frowned upon in their own society. The old woman always had available a supply of local men who could be counted on for discretion in the event a guest encountered them in the street. Dorian never knew whether they were paid to be here or if they too had developed a taste for forbidden fruit. Judging by the gleeful expressions on the faces of the two fellows filling the hind end of his neighbor, Dorian concluded it was the latter.

The young man whose mouth had been servicing him increased the pressure of his lips, determined to bring

Dorian to a conclusion, his fist moving up and down in his own lap in concert with his mouth as he likewise endeavored to bring pleasure to himself. Dorian had almost forgotten he was there, so caught up had he become in the events transpiring at his side. The youth reminded him of a young Omar, with his dark skin and eyes and hair like rippling black silk. Grabbing hold of his head, Dorian forced it lower until he felt the crown of his prick kissing the back of his pleasure-giver's throat. There was an audible gag at the intrusion, but no lull in the procedure; he merely readjusted the angle of his mouth so that he could swallow still more.

The poppy made Dorian feel as if he were floating in a warm underwater grotto. The young man's tongue was a soft fern lapping against the underside of his prick, the teeth above the jagged edges of a coral reef, the back of his throat the entrance to a secret cave. The slower his reflexes became, the faster the dark head moved, yet climax was still a long way from arriving. *Let the lad work for his pleasure*, he mused, his deep sigh attracting the attention of his female neighbor. Her opium-heavy eyes met his, her lips bursting open like a sunflower coming into bloom each time the men launched themselves inside her, their walnut-colored skin glistening from their efforts.

Dorian offered her a lazy smile. "Pray, turn toward me so that I may better savor your pleasure with my eyes," he said.

She laughed softly, the sound like the tinkling of bells. The music of it was as pretty as her face and Dorian felt a surge of blood to his prick; it wouldn't be long before the young man received his reward. "But do you not have enough pleasure to occupy yourself?" she teased, her eyes indicating the head bobbing to and fro in Dorian's lap. "The lad seems to be very hard at work. Surely you would not wish to neglect him by turning your attention elsewhere? How frightfully mean-spirited that would be!" Hearing this, the young man's eyes strained upward, staring at Dorian in panic, as if fearing he might disengage himself and go elsewhere.

The young woman's accent was as cultivated and English as Dorian's. It amused him to think that he might have known her in society, had he still been living in London. "Indeed, my dear, but can one ever have too much pleasure?"

"Perhaps not," she concurred. "In that case, I should not wish to deprive you." With a devastating smile that inflamed Dorian's lust still further, she shifted toward him, prompting the other two participants to do likewise until the nucleus of activity was directly before him. Rather than gazing on the lovely oval of her face, Dorian was presented with another oval being stretched well beyond the circumference nature intended. Had he not indulged so liberally in the poppy, he might have offered himself as a third party in the proceedings. Yet even if he'd wished to, he could not have moved; his arms and legs were weighted to the floor.

The young lady began to peak, her fingers digging jagged tracks of blood along her thighs that looked like the juicy red of pomegranate seeds against her pale flesh. It was followed by tormented groans from the men as first one, then the other, discharged their pleasure inside her, their erect flesh popping out of her like corks from a champagne bottle. As the three collapsed together in a jumble of dark and light, Dorian filled the mouth in his lap, tumbling into unconsciousness immediately after.

He slept for he knew not how long, but it was a deep and untroubled sleep—indeed, one of the most peaceful he'd experienced in some while. When he awakened, he discovered a servant hovering over him holding out a tray with hot fragrant tea and a bowl with brown lumps of sugar. Placing it on the floor, he disappeared as discreetly as he'd appeared. Dorian wondered how the fellow managed not to be affected by the activities that had gone on in the room and were continuing to go on by those who had already risen.

The sweetness of the sugar and the warmth of the liquid roused Dorian into full wakefulness. Dawn had already broken over the city. It was time for him to return to his own bed and sleep away the day. He felt better than he had in weeks, as if every unpleasant memory had been flushed from his veins. Lord and Lady Oadby's dogged pursuit of him now seemed like something he'd imagined—the result of some silly paranoia brought on by Omar's death. Dorian found himself laughing at his folly for allowing himself to get into such a state about it.

Stretching languorously, he propelled himself up from the floor. At some point in the night he had mislaid his trousers. Fortunately he still wore his gandora; he ran his palms down the front to make it more presentable, relieved to discover that its pocket still contained the key to his house. The garment was of sufficient length to cover his modesty; he should be able to travel through the streets without attracting undue attention until he had safely reached his front gate.

The Englishwoman and her two male companions still lay in a tangled tableau of limbs, their breathing indicating they were fast asleep. Something told Dorian he would be seeing her here again—*and* that she would be eager to accept his advances. Making his way from the room, he passed an elderly man and woman slumped in a corner. Their heads lolled on their necks as if they'd met with the hangman's noose. Dorian might have thought the old gentleman dead but for the terrible rattling and wheezing emanating from his chest. His scrawny form was naked save for a partially buttoned woolen waistcoat with a gold timepiece hanging from a chain. His female companion wore a dress in the local style, though her fair skin and hair indicated that she wasn't native to the area. The garment was in a considerable state of disarray, as were the woman's chubby legs, which were splayed like those of a Christmas goose waiting to be stuffed.

Suddenly Dorian realized that he knew her. *And* he knew her companion.

The sense of well-being that had greeted him on awakening was gone. This could be no coincidence—Lord and Lady Oadby had followed him here. For all he knew, they had been observing his activities for the entire night until he'd dropped off to sleep. But what had occurred after that? Had they come upon his slumbering form and used it for their own purposes? Knowing them as he did, he would not have put it past them. He felt his fingers clenching into deadly fists. Perhaps he should kill them right where they slept, squeezing the life from their throats until nothing remained but their withered husks. At least then he'd be free to roam the streets again. Instead he hurried toward the sour-smelling stairwell and out into the freshness of morning. For Dorian there was no enjoyment in the clean sunshine that washed over his face or in the spice-scented air that purged the odors of stale sex and smoke from his nostrils. There was only the sense that time was quickly running out.

From then on Dorian refused to leave his house. He remained sequestered inside his shadowy bedroom, smoking opium and listening to the calls to prayer from the muezzin, each one seeming to chastise him for his wickedness and godlessness. He no longer even took proper meals, preferring to eat only dates washed down with glass after glass of heavily sugared tea until he felt as if his teeth would rot.

Shortly afterward the dreams began—or rather *The Dream*, as he was coming to think of it. It always featured the same woman. She was young and beautiful, with hair and eyes like honey gleaming in the sunlight. Her lips possessed the ripeness of summer cherries; he swore he could taste their sweetness in his sleep. She was smiling, her eyes bright and pure with love, her expression free of guile. Dorian sensed that *he* was the cause of such female joy and it made him feel happy and carefree—the kind of carefree that only a boy still innocent of the world's evils can truly know. Had Dorian ever been such a boy? Yet here, in The Dream, he was.

The love flowing toward him from this young woman was not the same as the love he'd been given by others. It did not suffocate or make demands or carry with it a sense of guilt or disappointment. This was a different kind of love—a love he welcomed with his entire being, a love that had the power to clean his corrupted soul of its filth. It reached down to him from the heavens, bringing only goodness and purity. How dearly Dorian longed for this love and all that it promised!

But each time he awakened, there were only the shadows in the darkened room from which he rarely ventured pulling him into their embrace, dragging him down to Hell.

He blamed the poppy. Its overuse was causing him to suffer hallucinations in his sleep, then leaving him in a stupor for his waking hours. He was turning into Omar, yet what else was there for him? He dared not step outside the walls surrounding his house for fear of encountering the Oadbys. He knew they were there—he could smell them like a cornered animal smells its predator.

He needed to go somewhere so distant that no one would ever find him.

PERU,
196—

We are punished for our refusals. Every impulse that we strive to strangle broods in the mind and poisons us.

—Lord Henry Wotton

Dorian lived the life of a nomad, never remaining for long in one location. He journeyed by train and ship and even donkey cart. Whatever means were at his disposal took him farther away from the past; the luxury of the conveyance was of no consequence. It was more important to keep moving than to enjoy the scenery—at least until he felt safe. The sense of being hunted plagued him; he frequently caught himself checking over his shoulder, as if he might see the Oadbys or someone else from the past sneaking up behind him.

When his despair was at its darkest, he saw Omar—and it was *not* the young, handsome Omar from the alleyway, but the poppy-addicted Omar with the circles of soot beneath his eyes and the betraying marks of decay that had caused his soul to burn with hatred each time he looked at the eternally youthful man upon whose charity he lived. Had Dorian not killed Omar, Omar would have one day killed *him*.

Dorian remained as flawless as ever. He knew that no matter where he went, this situation would repeat itself; therefore he adopted a more primitive form of existence. He neither mingled in society nor engaged with others, save for acquiring the basic necessities of life. He passed nearly two decades in this fashion, reaching places as far-flung as India and the southernmost end of Peru, where he decided to remain for a while. The years had gone by slowly and he felt the tedium of each one, not to mention the anguish of extinguishing his desires like a fire doused by a torrent of cold water. There were no more salacious reports following him from country to country and continent to continent, leading to his whereabouts like a trail of breadcrumbs. Since fleeing Marrakesh Dorian had avoided establishments catering to the more debauched members of society, knowing that even a small taste of such delights would propel him back into his old life. Instead he fought the urge for fleshly sensation until he believed he would go mad, finding a perverse enjoyment in self-deprivation that added to his repertoire of sensations.

The war in Europe had ended, leaving behind ravaged landscapes and countless casualties. But his native England had endured. Dorian wondered if he would ever set foot upon its shores again. Was there anyone left alive whom he had once known? He thought of Lord Henry and the last time he'd seen him, which had been the evening he'd relayed with such naïve pride his sparing of Hettie Merton's chastity.

"Play me a nocturne, Dorian, and, as you play, tell me in a low voice how you have kept your youth," Lord Henry had said. "You must have some secret. I am only ten years older than you are, and I am wrinkled and bald and yellow."

Only ten years older.

Even back then it was difficult to imagine so small a number separating them in age, when the eye declared otherwise. Could dear Harry still be alive somewhere in the world at this very moment? Dorian hoped it to be so. The man had been like a father, a lover, a god. Although at the end he had disappointed him, Lord Henry was the closest Dorian had ever been to another human being—and this had given Dorian a curious sense of belonging he had never experienced since.

Dorian settled for a time in a quiet valley located in the shadow of a volcano in the south of Peru. To anyone in the village who asked—and with a population comprised exclusively of Quechuas there were enough who overcame their shyness to speak to him—Dorian claimed to be a man of faith who had come seeking spiritual enlightenment so that he might pass on his knowledge to others. This was how he'd first learned of a monastery located high up in the mountains. Its presence proved to be an unexpected bonus, since everyone believed this was why he'd chosen to come here. To add further credence to his tale, Dorian purchased a battered old typewriter from a shopkeeper in a nearby town, which he kept out on the scarred wooden table beneath the dusty window of his room in the event the old woman from whom he rented his lodgings called in when he was absent. He quite enjoyed his new persona and even spent some time typing away on the decrepit instrument, finding that his random entries would make a fine book after he was finished, particularly since they pertained mostly to the hedonistic philosophies in which Lord Henry had instructed him.

Had Dorian been anyone else, he might have been content with his new existence. Life had been pared down to a beautiful kind of simplicity, and for some it might have been enough. But the pressure of his lust had been building like the pressure inside the volcano that hovered over the valley; an explosion was imminent. The catalyst that finally triggered it would need to be masterfully executed, for he had to make up for many arid years of self-denial.

Donning the humble peasant's garb that had become his daily attire, Dorian set forth on foot for the mountains, looking like a man with nothing but the clothing on his back and only his wits to guide him. He had no purpose or destination in mind, yet his feet seemed to be leading him somewhere. The first night he slept rough, awakening as dusty and dirty as the impoverished beggars who occasionally traveled through the towns and villages. His shabby appearance, combined with a few words of Quechua, aided him well enough to locate a bed on the second night. The fact that it was located inside the monastery he had heard about gave rise to a plan that would be a masterpiece of corruption. It came to him the moment he saw the young monk working in the vineyards. The frank purity in the man's broad brown face cried out to Dorian to sully it.

At the monastery he was given a tiny cell-like room in which to sleep. The little cot that served as a bed proved as hard and unwelcoming as a boulder, but it inspired within Dorian thoughts of martyrdom, reinvigorating his former fascination with the Roman Catholic Church and men who lived lives devoid of fleshly pleasure. He spent a fitful first night, though it was not from discomfort in his accommodations, but instead from his mounting excitement over his intention to commit an act of sacrilege so hellishly divine he could smell the brimstone in his nostrils.

Dorian concocted a tale of misfortune and claimed to have no place else to turn; therefore the brothers agreed to let him stay. In return for their charity, he worked in the monastery gardens, either hoeing or planting or harvesting depending on the growing stage of the crop he was assigned to. He found such humble toil a pleasant novelty. Working with his hands out of doors within sight of young Brother Tomás brought its own special joy. The monk was not altogether ill-favored, with his dark brown eyes and smooth brown skin, though neither was he prepossessing. His cheekbones were too broad and his body too squat, as if his torso had been wedged atop his hips rather than being separated by a waistline. Yet when Dorian looked closer, he saw sparkling flecks of amber in the young monk's eyes that lit up his entire face like a candle glowing in a shadowy church nave. He was also blessed with very graceful hands, more like those of a skilled pianist than those of a man who worked the soil. As Dorian joined with the others in prayer—another requirement of his stay—he entertained himself with images of Brother Tomás's fingers encircling his prick and kneading it to its requisite conclusion. He wondered if the monk or any of his brothers did so to themselves or possibly even to each other. It seemed terribly unnatural for men to voluntarily pledge to abstain from all fleshly pleasures, whether they were delivered by the bodies of women or by themselves.

At the monastery Dorian did everything he could to make himself useful, going far beyond the tasks assigned to him in order to prove his worth and secure a home at the order until such time as he wished to leave. His work was still very far from being accomplished, though he'd been steadily gaining Brother Tomás's friendship and trust, engaging with him in philosophical discourse on such subjects as immortality and sin—subjects about which Dorian had a great deal of personal knowledge. He did his best to hide his amusement at the young monk's naïve opinions.

Tomás's inner fire was beginning to burn as they talked and debated long into the night in the monk's tiny room, which was nearly identical to the one Dorian had been assigned but for the added luxury of a chair in which to sit and reflect on the Scriptures. Dorian realized it was both an achievement and an honor for him to be invited into the monk's private quarters, for they were not intended for entertaining and socializing, but for prayer and sleep. That Dorian had an entirely new use planned for them was the only thing that prevented him from becoming overwhelmed by boredom. A gardener he would never be, unless one considered the planting of one's seed into a bodily orifice a form of *gardening*.

Although diffident when in a public space, in private Brother Tomás seemed almost boyish in his eagerness for companionship, confirming Dorian's belief that life at the monastery was a very lonely existence for a healthy young man. He'd detected little camaraderie among the other brothers and wasn't even certain of the protocol when it came to such matters as fraternizing. However, it soon became apparent that there was a definite pecking order at work—and Tomás appeared to be located in the lower stratum.

Eventually Dorian brought their discussions around to the subject of the flesh, beginning slowly by making a casual reference to the curious yearnings of his own body and inquiring whether young Tomás had ever experienced similar feelings. It was fortunate that the monk's knowledge of English was sufficiently advanced to allow for these discussions or else Dorian would have had to employ a less subtle approach that might have compromised his chances for success. "I have never been with a woman," he confided to Tomás one night, fighting the laughter that threatened to burst forth like a clap of thunder. "There is something terribly wicked in their bodies—and it frightens me that I shall face eternal damnation should I fall prey to it!"

Tomás nodded thoughtfully, as if such a notion were not altogether unfamiliar to him. "Yes," he replied softly, reaching for Dorian's hand in an attempt to reassure him. "I understand, Brother Dorian, truly I do."

Dorian had by this time made himself so invaluable to the daily workings of the monastery that he'd earned himself the respect and fraternity of being referred to as "Brother Dorian," even though he had not taken holy orders. Lord Henry would have made much merriment of it all, he mused, summoning tears to his eyes to further his visage of fear that his pure young body might be defiled by those belonging to sinful ladies.

"But sometimes I—" and here he faltered purposefully, waiting until Tomás leaned in closer to better hear his terrible confession.

Both men were seated cross-legged on the little cot facing one another and wearing the identical dark robes of the order; Dorian was rock-hard beneath his. It was all he could do to keep from throwing open the burdensome garment and exposing himself in his full glory to Brother Tomás's innocent eyes. "Oh, it is too shameful to utter!" he cried, bringing the hand the young monk continued to hold up to his cheek so that it could feel his tears.

Tomás looked into Dorian's eyes with kindness, the light from the oil lamp emphasizing the amber flecks. "Brother Dorian, perhaps it is best for you to speak of it so that you may cast it from your mind and heart and cleanse your soul!" His brown face was sincere in its pain. He'd often been told as a boy that his heart was too soft, which was one of the reasons why he had decided to seek out the brotherhood—to spare himself from the human heartache that afflicted so many when they allowed the desires of their bodies to rule.

Dorian produced a pitiful sob, the tears now coming in earnest, though they were tears of mirth rather than the tears of humiliation he wished Brother Tomás to believe them to be. Gulping as if his lungs were starved of oxygen, he finally managed to continue, speaking so softly the monk had to lean nearer still in order to hear him. "I believe it may be better to remain pure with another such as myself than to succumb to the sins of Eve."

Brother Tomás went deathly silent. Suddenly Dorian feared he had perhaps gone farther than he should have, especially this soon. Had he spoken too frankly before the monk was ready to listen? Cursing inwardly, he tried to think of a way to extricate himself from the situation. He'd invested a good deal of time and thought into his planned corruption of the young monk—he couldn't risk it failing now. Yet he didn't think he could keep a rein on his desires for much longer. He would either need to take Tomás by force, which, although an agreeable option, wouldn't prove nearly as satisfying as getting him to succumb, or he'd have to abandon his plan and be on his way.

When Tomás removed his hand from Dorian's grasp, the latter feared his worst assessment of the situation had come to pass. At that moment he expected the monk to not only order him from his room, but to call out to his brothers for assistance and have him thrown bodily into the black of night. Instead the younger man sat quietly, his broad features a study in conflict. When at last he spoke, Dorian wanted to embrace him in jubilation. "Brother Dorian, you speak sense."

Rather than risk doing anything to damage the tenuous link he'd been building between the monk and himself, Dorian kept silent, hoping the disturbance beneath his robe wouldn't give away his true objectives. His prick felt as if it would erupt like the volcano he'd been living in the shadow of. Indeed, some of his seed had already spilled, though there was still a plentiful supply remaining. If something did not happen between them before he returned to his room, Dorian would be forced to abuse himself with his own hand until sunrise. His desire to have the other man's unsullied lips upon his rigid flesh was such that he believed he would go mad from want. Brother Tomás was not fine-looking by anyone's definition, but he was pure and he had taken a vow of chastity. Dorian's need to defile this blessed purity made the monk a thing of beauty in his eyes.

"Perhaps we should continue our discussion another time, Brother Dorian. It is late and there is much work to be done tomorrow," said Tomás, no longer appearing conflicted, only matter-of-fact about the realities of daily life in a rural monastery.

"Yes, you are right, my dear brother," agreed Dorian, trying to hide his disappointment with an ingenuous smile. "I shall look forward to it." He bounded up from the cot and made for the door, keeping his back toward Tomás so that his erection would not be seen. "Till tomorrow night then!"

A short while later Dorian was back in his own cot, his hand working his prick with such vigor he thought the delicate skin would shred. No matter how many times he reached the terminus his relief was still not satisfactory. All he could think about was defiling the young monk in every manner possible—and doing so again and again until Hell had opened up and swallowed them both. The torment of wanting someone whom he could not have easily proved to be an entirely new sensation for Dorian—and the challenge of it made the prize all the more desirable.

More than a week went past before the opportunity for the two men to meet again privately and resume their discussion finally presented itself. Dorian's nightly ritual of self-abuse had become such a regular part of his routine that it pained him to even pass water. To add further insult, the days had grown disagreeably hot, making every task a struggle to perform. What little breeze there was had become tainted with an orange dust that coated the skin and clothing and crept into the corners of the eyes and nostrils. There was no relief to be found in the claustrophobic rooms of the monastery, where the nights proved even more wretched, since by then the day's work had been completed and there was nothing remaining but to lie in frustration either waiting for sleep or waiting, as Dorian was, for a sign that he could take matters to the next step with Brother Tomás.

It was clear that the young monk was having a difficult time as well. Dorian discerned from the fatigue on Tomás's face that he too appeared to be suffering from restless nights, though he hoped the cause was owing to the monk's arousal from the nature of their conversations than the unpleasantness of the weather. Finally Dorian decided to test his theory, for he could not stand idly by any longer. After evening prayer he went directly up to Brother Tomás and suggested they meet later that night. He was delighted when his proposal was eagerly accepted.

Earlier that day they had both been working in the vineyard—and this provided Dorian with a neutral venue in which to take matters in the direction he most wanted them to go. The two were seated side by side on the monk's cot, their backs leaning against the stone wall and their sandaled feet dangling over the side. Tomás had been expressing his concern over the recent infestation of pests due to the hot weather, inadvertently providing Dorian with the opening he sought. Sighing heavily, Dorian made a dramatic show of wiping his brow with his sleeve. "I am finding this heat most oppressive," he said, fidgeting uncomfortably in his robe. "I am not certain I can bear it for much longer!"

"Yes, it is truly awful!" Brother Tomás concurred. "I find sleep impossible at this time of year."

Dorian nodded thoughtfully, as if considering the problem and seeking a solution for it. "Brother Tomás, I do not believe we should be made to suffer like this."

"What choice do we have? God has sent us this weather and we must make the best of it."

"Even so, our suffering is unnecessary."

"What do you mean, Brother Dorian?"

"These robes—they are suffocating us in this heat!"

"But they are all we have. It is what we have always worn." Tomás appeared bewildered by what he took to be a criticism of the brothers' established mode of dress.

"Of course—and under normal circumstances when we are out and about doing God's work our garments are perfectly suitable! But it is now just the two of us here in your room, chatting as friends. Surely there is no need for formality here?"

"Then what would you suggest we do?"

"I suggest we make ourselves more comfortable while we are conversing," Dorian replied sensibly. "After all, it is very private and no one will see us." Pushing the hood of his robe further back from his head, he raked his fingers through the damp curls, the sensation of his own touch giving rise to goose flesh on his body. Rising from the cot, he began to unfasten the rope at the waist of his garment, hoping that Brother Tomás would follow suit and do the same. Yet the monk continued to remain seated, regarding him with uncertainty.

Just as Dorian grasped hold of the lower half of his robe in readiness to pull it up over his head, Tomás cried out: "What are you doing, Brother Dorian? Surely this is not correct!"

Dorian looked down at the monk with an expression of such purity that even the most suspicious of souls would have been unable to detect a hint of the vice that dwelled in his heart. "But why ever not, dear brother?" he asked in astonishment. "Surely God does not wish for us to suffer in this heat any more than we're already suffering!"

Tomás appeared to be considering the sense of this; eventually the doubt clouding his features vanished. "Yes, you are right, Brother Dorian. How foolish of me. Please forgive me."

"There is nothing to forgive, dear Tomás!" Smiling reassuringly, Dorian proceeded to pull his robe the remainder of the way over his head, allowing it to drop to the floor at his feet. The air caressing his bare skin was like a splash of cool river water on a sun-heated bank as he stood naked before the monk, having removed his trousers in advance of his visit.

A strangled gasp came from the cot as the glow from the oil lamp revealed to the monk's disbelieving eyes the perfection of Dorian's form. Dorian's prick rose up from his loins, bobbing heavily against his belly as if seeking to draw attention to itself, the bead of moisture at the tip providing further evidence of his secret need. Brother Tomás trembled discernibly despite the warmth in the room, seeming unable to move.

Stretching languidly as if awakening from a pleasurable sleep, Dorian turned to the side to better showcase his manhood. He knew from his sessions of self-admiration before the mirror that it was equally impressive in silhouette and he wished to make certain young Tomás's eyes had been given their fill. "There! I feel refreshed already!" he declared, as if it were perfectly natural for an adult male to display his fully erect manhood to a monk. "You must agree this is far more practical. Do get those dreadful garments off, Brother Tomás. They are positively suffocating!"

"I—I am not certain that I can," the monk faltered, his dark eyes locked on Dorian's prick.

"Do not be shy!" chided Dorian. "For we are brothers, are we not?"

Tomás swallowed hard, the noise resounding in the tiny room like a gunshot, his face darkening with the embarrassed stain of his blush. "I—" he sounded on the verge of tears. His hands fidgeted in his lap like a pair of caged birds that, even when presented with the possibility of release, remained hesitant as to whether or not to accept it.

After turning in a slow circle so that he could be admired from every angle, Dorian stood facing Tomás and offered him a gentle smile. "Is it not silly to reject the natural state as something *unnatural*?" he asked, his tone encouraging. "Think of Michelangelo's David. Was he not a thing of great beauty?" Inspired by his own words, Dorian replicated the graceful pose of the famous sculpture. Indeed, there were moments when he amazed himself with his own brilliance; this was one of them.

Brother Tomás continued to stare at Dorian's erect flesh, as if he had never seen something of its nature, his body quaking with an emotion that not even he could identify. The amber flecks in his eyes burned bright enough to compete with the lamplight illuminating Dorian's prick.

Dorian stepped forward until its moistened crown was at the same level as the monk's mouth. Reaching out his hand as if to befriend a frightened dog, he caressed Tomás's burning cheek, finding it wet with tears. His excitement at being so close to the realization of his profane plan made him fear that he would spray his seed all over the young man's face. Although that contained its own delightful element of profanity, it was Dorian's intention for Brother Tomás to take him into his mouth until he had swallowed every drop of his pleasure.

Time had slowed down in the stifling little room. The sound of their rapid breathing became amplified, adding to the oppressive heat. Dorian smelled the musky aroma of his armpits and loins and knew that Brother Tomás smelled it too, especially at such close range. It was an intoxicating odor that never failed to arouse him, whether it came from his own body or another man's. He could tell that it was having an effect on the monk by the dilation of his nostrils. He moved closer still until his erection was almost touching Tomás's lips—all Tomás needed to do was open them.

Dorian waited, his patience turning to irritation as Tomás remained frozen in place on the cot. The night grew heavier outside the walls of the monastery, as did the pressure in Dorian's testes as his body screamed for release. Although he'd known the seduction would not be easy, he had yet to meet a man or woman who'd not succumbed in the end. That this damn fool of a cleric should be immune to him or capable of ignoring the desires that stirred in his heart was beyond imagining. It was all Dorian could do to refrain from forcing himself on Tomás to be granted his relief. But for his master plan to be properly executed, the young monk needed to become a willing partner in his desecration. Reining in his impatience, Dorian tenderly cupped the back of Tomás's head before guiding it forward. When he felt the monk's lips parting he all but cheered in victory. Indeed, had he done so, it would have roused every monk from his bed. The image of them charging like crazed bulls into Brother Tomás's room to rescue him from danger was a most diverting image and one which Dorian later took to his cot for one last bout of pleasure before he slept.

That night left Brother Tomás crumpled into a ball on his cot, sobbing and flailing at himself in condemnation. He had succeeded in performing the function Dorian had required of him. There had been moments of hesitation, but he eventually overcame them, demonstrating a talent for the act that had surprised him as much as it had surprised its recipient. To the monk's mortification, he did not even turn away from the finale. Though it had left him sputtering and coughing, Tomás allowed nothing to go to waste, the seemingly endless flow of Dorian's pleasure onto his tongue mirroring his own as it soiled the interior of his robe, adding to his shame and confusion.

Dorian had expected they would resume their activities the following night, but when he went to call on Brother Tomás in his room, discovered him absent. He slipped inside to wait, stripping off his robe and lying on the cot, palming his erection to better prepare it for what was to come. But the monk never showed. And so it would be each night after until Dorian became convinced that he was being played for a fool.

As for the day, he no longer saw Tomás working in the vineyards. It was strictly by chance that he learned the monk had been reassigned to the monastery kitchens. This sounded like a rather curious duty for a man of his ilk, Brother Tomás's talents having always lain in the agricultural pursuits rather than the domestic. He had once told Dorian that he'd come to the brothers directly from the farm—the prospect of him spending his hours chopping vegetables and frying meat made little sense. Was he sleeping in the kitchens as well? For he had still not returned to his room.

The possibility of speaking with Tomás under these circumstances, let alone orchestrating a rendezvous, had now become severely restricted. The kitchen was a busy place and did not allow for the intimacy of private conversation. As for an opportunity of catching the monk elsewhere, even when they took their meals he would always make sure to sit at the opposite end of the refectory table, with no vacant chairs on either side or across from him. It was clear to Dorian that Tomás was avoiding him.

Was one quick act of defilement to be the full extent of his victory?

He decided to lie in wait—Brother Tomás couldn't hide from him forever! The opportunity for a confrontation finally presented itself one Sunday after morning service in the chapel. Dorian spied the monk making his way outside through a side door. He hurried after him so as not to lose sight of his robed form—the property was vast, providing many places in which one could vanish. He followed Tomás past the vineyards, then past the barrel room, and still the young man kept going, his gait determined. Perhaps he intended to walk to the village, though a Sunday morning was unlikely to provide much in the way of amusement even for a simple monk. Dorian continued his pursuit, keeping far enough back that his presence wouldn't be detected, though Tomás never once turned to look behind him.

As they drew near the village, Brother Tomás veered in the opposite direction, proceeding up a hill. By now Dorian's curiosity was burning a hole in his head. As far as he was aware, there was nothing up this way but miles of untamed land. That the monk or *anyone* should desire to come here made no sense; the growing heat of the day made the journey as arduous as the ascent. The land became increasingly steep and cluttered with vegetation, proving a challenge for Dorian to keep his pursuit a secret. Several times along the way he nearly lost his footing but managed to right himself without attracting notice. Eventually they reached the summit, which gave way to a small clearing. Here the monk stopped.

Taking shelter behind a tree, Dorian waited to see what would happen next. He wondered if Brother Tomás might be waiting for someone and felt a stab of jealous anger in his belly. Could this be why the monk had been avoiding him? Perhaps he had arranged for an assignation with a whore from the village—or worse, another monk from the monastery. What other purpose could he have for choosing such an out-of-the-way location?

Dorian felt his fingernails breaking through the skin of his palms as his hands clenched into fists. Had all his careful grooming of the young monk led to the spoils of victory being stolen by another? Blood would surely be shed if this were the case, though he'd make certain to take his pleasure first—he had earned it.

Standing in the center of the clearing, Brother Tomás raised up his arms to embrace the heavens, only to instead tear the dark robe from his body as if its mere touch burned his flesh. Casting the garment onto the ground, he stepped out of his trousers, kicking them away in disgust as though he'd soiled them. For several minutes he simply stood there, his nakedness exposed to the world. He did not act in any way like a man who was expecting someone. On the contrary, it quickly became evident that Brother Tomás believed himself to be very much alone.

As the midday sun shone down upon the monk's squat body, he grasped hold of the brown tube of flesh dangling below his belly and began to squeeze and stroke it until it had become fully energized. His lips moved in a rhythmic pattern that seemed to be replicating that of his hand, carrying to Dorian's ear a mumbled prayer—a prayer seeking forgiveness for one's sins. As Tomás's hand moved faster, the murmuring was replaced by the amplified sound of his respiration, which became increasingly ragged as if each breath were being ripped from his chest. "Dorian!" he cried into the sky, his stocky buttocks clenching as his ejaculate watered the soil at his feet. Collapsing to his knees, he sobbed wretchedly as if every misery of the world had been laid at his doorstep.

Brother Tomás's performance did not leave Dorian unaffected. He too spent himself. He was astonished by what he'd just witnessed and wondered what Lord Henry would have made of it all. There were moments when he could sense Harry's presence, as if his mentor was looking on and offering encouragement. At times it was so real that he could smell his opium-tainted cigarettes. He could smell them now, even here in the outdoors among the trees and vegetation and the musky sweat being carried toward him on the air from the monk's body. He also smelled victory.

Although Tomás continued to avoid Dorian at the monastery, every Sunday after morning prayer he undertook the journey to the clearing atop the hill—as did Dorian, who believed it was only a matter of time before the monk returned to occupy his room and await his nocturnal caller. Brother Tomás's sexual torment was a beauty to behold. He abused himself beneath the sun's unrelenting spotlight, his thick-set form wracked by sobs and the expulsion of his climax as the name of the man who caused his anguish echoed over the hilltops, blending with the sighs of the wind. Dorian had now taken to joining him, timing it so that they both reached the pinnacle together. Though the temptation to make his presence known was a continual battle, he forced himself to wait, since he was enjoying the development of his master plan far too much to tamper with it. For rather than Dorian defiling the monk, the monk was defiling himself.

This exquisite irony fed Dorian's hunger for sensation and gave rise to new inspirations, one of which included writing a humble letter of apology designed to put Tomás off his guard and fuel his guilt-ridden desires until his desperation for relief tore away the last scraps of his chastity, leaving him defenseless and open to accept the act of sacrilege from which there could be no return. Dorian slipped the letter inside the monk's prayer book, left momentarily unattended in the chapel, Lord Henry's laughter resounding in his ears.

My dear Brother Tomás,

Pray forgive me if I have committed some grave misdeed that has sent you into hiding!

I know not what I may have done, but if I have in some manner offended or upset you, please trust in me when I say it was never my intent to cause upset.

I am but a simple man unskilled in the ways of the world. I have been traveling for a very long time, wishing only to find my way and live a life of goodness and charity. When the brothers took me in, I truly believed that my lonely journey had at last come to an end. Here among you I have found fraternity and a higher calling—indeed, I have found a reason to live! I know I am not one of you; I have not taken my vows before God or pledged my life to serving Him. But these things are in my heart, and I know that they are in yours. So you see, we are brothers!

Dearest Tomás, you have so much to teach me and I am so eager to learn! When we are together it is as if I am home. There is no pretense or formality between us—and this is as it should be with those of our kind. More than anything I miss our nightly discussions. For it is during these times when I feel my soul being raised to a higher plane—and it is all thanks to you, my cherished friend! My devotion to you as my teacher and companion knows no bounds. My poor heart is weighed down with grief with the passing of each day that does not bring us together again.

Tomás, I am lost and barren without your wisdom and guidance. Please end my suffering and allow me back into the kind and loving embrace of your friendship!

Ever yours on Earth and in Heaven,
Brother Dorian

The next night Brother Tomás resumed occupancy of his room. Dorian, finding the door ajar, found himself somewhat disappointed that Tomás had caved in so quickly, for this was clearly an invitation intended for no one but him. The brothers did not call upon one another in the nighttime hours, which they reserved for quiet reflection and sleep. When Dorian received no response to his light tapping, he urged the door open further and peered inside. Tomás was seated upon his cot, his demeanor anxious, though when his eyes eventually rose to meet Dorian's they burned with a fire that told of a lifetime of suppressed desires. Seeing the raw need tormenting the young monk's soul prompted Dorian's prick to twitch eagerly beneath his robe. "Brother Tomás, might I be allowed to enter?" he asked, suppressing his laughter at the delicious double meaning behind his words.

The monk nodded, indicating that his guest could join him on the cot. Closing the door behind him, Dorian settled himself beside Tomás, surprised to find his heartbeat accelerating as their thighs brushed together. He would need to move gently in order to regain the young man's trust, though after the letter he had written he imagined this was but a formality—another step in a slow dance of seduction. Remembering the utter claptrap he'd penned onto paper was enough to bring on another threat of laughter and he turned away to hide the grin splitting his face. "I trust you are well, Brother Tomás?" he at last managed to say.

When the monk did not respond, Dorian repeated his question. When Tomás finally spoke, his voice was barely above a whisper. "Yes, Brother Dorian. I am well," he replied, sounding and looking anything but. Dark circles had taken up residence beneath his eyes, and the lids above were puffy and red as if he'd been rubbing them with his fists.

"My dear brother, have you not been sleeping? Forgive me for saying this, but you appear most out of sorts!"

Tomás nodded sadly. "A great burden has been preying upon me. I fear it has kept me from my rest."

"Indeed?" Dorian's eyebrows lifted into a question. "But what ever can it be that is burdening you so? Surely it is not so grave as you imagine!"

"I dare not even speak of it. It is too shameful!" Tomás hung his head in disgrace as if he'd already confessed to his caller every last one of his sins. "Oh, Brother Dorian, how I suffer!"

"I cannot bear to see you in such misery. No, it simply will not do! You are too good and kind—"

Tomás hid his face in his hands and began to weep. The twitching beneath Dorian's robe turned into an unwieldy erection as he moved to console the monk, pulling him into his embrace and rocking him as if he were a child. Considering the proximity of their bodies, it had to be impossible for Tomás *not* to feel Dorian's rigid flesh burrowing into his belly, yet he made no attempt to pull away. "My dear friend, it does not nourish the soul to keep a burden to oneself," said Dorian. "A burden is meant to be shared until it is no longer a burden." Once again he fought to keep back his laughter. How in Heaven did he conceive of such banalities? Or perhaps how in *Hell* would be more fitting under the circumstances.

Brother Tomás curled into Dorian's chest seeking sanctuary, the hot scent of his skin palpable beneath his robe. The increasing pressure of his belly against Dorian's prick was exquisite, particularly since he had forgone wearing trousers. He was as hard and unyielding as stone and throbbed with the agony of a man who has waited far too long to claim his prize. "There, there," he comforted, drawing the monk even deeper into his arms. Despite the fact that Dorian had begun to urge his prick against him in a rhythmic motion, Tomás still made no move to get away. "You can trust me," he whispered, his voice a beautiful instrument of seduction. "Unburden yourself to me, dear Tomás. There is to be no shame between us."

Dorian was moments away from a climax when Tomás struggled to free himself. He leapt up from the cot, his face flushed and perspiring, his eyes wild as he stared at Dorian in horror. "What—" He seemed unable to complete the sentence.

Dorian cursed himself for once again allowing his impatience to get the better of him. Yet how could he have read the situation so wrongly? Was the monk still struggling between his desires and his faith and, perhaps even more so, the threat of discovery? Was that what the solitary performances on the hilltop were about—a way to relieve his disreputable torment safely out of sight from the eyes of the brothers? Although Dorian could have taken him there at any time, he wanted him here in the monastery, where Brother Tomás's ultimate desecration would be all the more poignant in its significance.

As Dorian reached out a hand in an attempt at appeasement, Tomás threw off his robe. He stood before Dorian in the thin trousers the brothers wore beneath their robes, a large erection straining against the fabric. Suddenly he flung himself facedown onto the cot. "Take me, Brother Dorian!" he cried wretchedly. "I do not know or understand what it is that I ask, but I beg for you to take me!"

Grabbing hold of the monk's trousers at the waist, Dorian yanked them down to his ankles, the cloth ripping and popping as he did so. The sound reverberated in the claustrophobic room, adding to the drama of the moment as Tomás's sturdy buttocks quivered in fear, the brown skin prickling as if hit by a chill wind. Dorian palmed them open, bringing into exposure the monk's secret shame. It looked unsullied and untested, much as he'd expected it would, and Dorian felt a surge of power electrify his prick at the realization that he had been invited—nay, *begged*—to alter its pristine state.

Stripping off his robe, Dorian allowed the tension and anticipation to build. He had to make certain the magnitude of what Brother Tomás wanted had registered in his mind. The monk needed to have full culpability in his decision to move forward with what was about to transpire, knowing that what he desired from Dorian was a sin that went beyond all sins.

Brother Tomás lay compliantly on the cot, giving no indication that he wished to flee, though he trembled despite the temperature in the room and the heat radiating from their naked bodies. Dorian spat into the opening beneath him, the crudeness of it causing the monk to flinch. He thought it added a nice touch to the occasion and he recalled with fondness how degraded it always made him feel when Omar had done likewise, though he had done so more as a statement of his contempt rather than attending to such niceties as preparing for entry. Without further warning, Dorian fell upon the prone figure, hearing a sharp cry as he took aim. There was no going back now for either of them.

The monk opened to Dorian as surely as the gates to Hell were opening to him, its fires burning his erect flesh to cinders as he slid inside. He had expected resistance, but the other man's passion clearly overrode his physical limitations. "Confess, Brother Tomás—confess to me what it is you desire!" he demanded, holding back from the last devastating thrust.

Tomás hammered his fists at the scratchy bedding, his lower half caught in the torturous limbo between teasing and complete ruination. "I confess, I confess!"

"But to *what* do you confess? I must hear you say it!"

The monk began to weep, his words strangling him. "I cannot!"

"But you must, Brother Tomás!"

"I beg of you not to make me say it! It is too shameful!"

"There is no shame here, brother," Dorian purred into his flushed ear, pressing forward another destructive inch. The monk was getting tight—the final breaking would be painful. He slipped his hand beneath Tomás's belly, meeting with rigid flesh. Encircling it with his fingers, he gave it a cruel squeeze. "Tell me what you want!"

By now the monk was sobbing uncontrollably,

sounding as though he couldn't breathe when he gave voice to his desires. "I—I want you to pass through the gates of Sodom!" he cried, the primal desperation in his voice a symphony to Dorian's ears.

"And so I shall, my dear brother!" Putting his full weight behind the definitive thrust, Dorian destroyed what remained of Brother Tomás's physical, emotional and spiritual purity. The act possessed the finality of death; for the young monk there could be no returning to what he'd once been.

Dorian took Tomás with no thought for tenderness or mercy or pleasure, though the animal groans the monk attempted to hide in his pillow indicated such callousness was not unwelcome. The smell of sweat and brimstone filled the tiny room, fogging the air like smoke from a censer. The atmosphere felt weighted; even the ceiling seemed to be pressing down upon them, seeking to crush their rutting bodies as if the walls of the monastery sought to punish them for committing sacrilege.

Dorian held back from completing the deed, savoring the delicious moments of Brother Tomás's humiliating fall from grace as if they were a fine meal. When at last he permitted his pleasure to arrive, it did so in a kaleidoscope of colored light that spun in circles around his head as he filled the monk with a liquid blessing that came straight from Lucifer's prick. Tomás quaked beneath him as his own private torment spilled into Dorian's hand, joining the ranks of the damned, his futile mumblings of a prayer for forgiveness adding to Dorian's triumph. "Pray to my cock, Brother Tomás," he taunted. "For it is your god now!"

After it was over, they remained locked together on

the cot, as if neither could bear to break their bond of blasphemy. When Dorian finally withdrew from the monk, he expected to discover his flesh scorched black and blistered from the fires of Hell, but even the smell of brimstone had gone. Wiping himself on the monk's discarded robe, he dressed and returned to his room.

Dorian Gray had no fear of Hell. For him Hell was located inside a concrete bunker in the English countryside, a place he planned never to go again. But Brother Tomás *did* have a fear of Hell—and he knew with certainty that a place had already been reserved there for him. It was simply a matter of how soon he'd be arriving.

The seasons came and went mostly unnoticed by Tomás, who no longer saw the beauty in nature or in much of anything. He only saw his own willing participation in his eternal damnation. For Dorian's part in the proceedings he could not truly cast blame; the Englishman had demanded nothing of him that he did not wish to provide. Their physical encounters were at once sacred and profane, beyond anything the monk could purge with prayer. Although he continued to seek forgiveness—often several times a day—he knew it was hopeless. Instead he allowed Dorian to use him in any manner he desired, at any time of the day or night, the word "no" never once passing from his lips. It was as if the other man held some power over him that no amount of faith or prayer could drive away. No matter how sinful and wrong the act, Tomás was always willing to comply. Little by little he felt his soul being eaten away as if by a disease, rotting inside his body until he could smell it on his skin and in his breath. Yet he didn't want to stop. To stop would have meant his death.

"Why do you do this?" he'd asked after Dorian debased him in the vestry after Morning Prayer.

"Because I can." The pure plainness of the answer was such that Tomás felt like a simpleton for asking the question.

"But you will go to Hell!"

Dorian had laughed so loud the monk feared they would be discovered. "My dear Brother Tomás, I am already there."

It was this very threat of discovery that Dorian seemed determined to provoke. No longer did he confine their activities exclusively to Tomás's room in the cloak of night, after everyone had retired to their beds. He had grown weary of such things as discretion—he wanted to take his relationship with the monk to a new level, choosing locations where the likelihood of being seen by others was at its highest. How foolish he'd been to deprive himself of the joys of exposure. It was as though Lord Henry were at his side, scolding him for his caution and reminding him that life was not best lived in the shadows.

In the full light of day Dorian bent Brother Tomás forward, taking him in the vineyards where anyone passing could see them. The threat of discovery added an entirely new sensation to his repertoire, heightening his pleasure while deepening the monk's shame and sense of sin. Should they be seen, there was nothing for Dorian to fear. He would doubtless be told to leave, but Brother Tomás would be thoroughly disgraced and cast out of the monastery—and perhaps out of the Church itself. Such penalties were heavy for a young peasant farmhand with nowhere to go and no one to take pity on him.

If the worst should occur, the expelled monk could always make his way to the city and use his newly acquired talents to support himself. Dorian thought he would do quite well; it would surely be an improvement over the life he led in this stifling prison of the frustrated and pious. He taunted the monk with this fate whenever he wished to add another dash of spice to their encounters. "Brother Tomás, you will become a very successful man should you decide to sell your backside in the city. Indeed, your clients will be lining up! But a word of advice: be prudent about offering free samples. You wouldn't want to tarnish your reputation by giving the impression that you're selling inferior goods."

"Oh, why must you degrade me so?" sobbed the young monk, crumbling like a dried leaf as he visualized the sordid future awaiting him once his sins were made public. And Tomás had no doubt that they would be.

"*Degrade you?* My dear brother, it is not *I* who degrade you. It is *you* who degrade yourself. You are the one bending over to offer yourself to me. Why, if you could bend any lower your nose would be touching your toes! As for my role in all this," here Dorian paused for dramatic effect, "I am merely a pawn made helpless by the Devil's temptation."

And so it went again and again, with Dorian placing the blame on Brother Tomás's overburdened shoulders until he eventually believed himself to be solely at fault. The blue of Brother Dorian's eyes was as pure as a summer sky and therefore did not lie. He had come to the brothers seeking shelter and protection, only to have his flesh corrupted and his chance to enter Heaven compromised. Tomás had caused Dorian's ruin just as surely as he'd caused his own.

The monk became convinced that he was possessed by a demon—perhaps by Beelzebub himself. He continued to engage in deeds that blackened his soul and earned him a place in Hell, each more blasphemous than the last, until it seemed there was no moment of the day or night when he wasn't committing some evil of the flesh. For Tomás there was no longer even a chance of Purgatory—his journey had only one destination. He was the Antichrist sent to corrupt the innocent. Having now corrupted Dorian, would he next prey upon his other brothers? Were they all to drop before him like fallen soldiers?

Brother Tomás became a ghost of the strong young man he'd once been. The circles beneath his eyes darkened still further, the lids growing puffier and redder until he looked like a fish that had been left to rot in the sun. His boxy figure became thin and bony, his once-sturdy chest and buttocks taking on a caved-in appearance, as if the flesh had been gouged out with a shovel. He rarely slept, owing to his accommodation of Dorian's appetites at all hours; there was rarely a time when his manhood was not standing up against his belly, demanding to take its pleasure. The more misery and humiliation it inflicted, the more the monk begged to be given still more.

However, when Dorian succeeded in violating him on the church altar only minutes after Mass had ended, Brother Tomás finally reached the end.

Dorian gazed out his window at the volcano. Its usual steam had increased since he'd been away, giving him cause for concern that an eruption might be forthcoming. Perhaps he'd stopped here long enough. He longed for something new, something exciting, something even more deliciously evil than what he'd already tasted. His work here was done.

Brother Tomás's body had been discovered in the clearing atop the hill he used to visit before his relationship with Dorian had begun in earnest. Were it not for Dorian's helpful suggestion that the brothers go in this direction—for he had often spied the young monk walking this way on a Sunday—Tomás would probably still be up there being pecked over by crows and other scavengers. A knife from the monastery kitchen was found by his side; Tomás had used it to sever the artery in his left wrist until he'd finally bled to death. The fact that he was found lying naked on the blood-soaked earth with his rigor-stiffened fingers clutching his shriveled manhood was, in Dorian's mind, a master stroke and one fitting the monk's end. Indeed, it was a magnum opus of death, as were the dried splotches of seminal fluid on Brother Tomás's chest and belly, which his fellow brothers pretended not to see before one of them volunteered his robe to cover the body.

How Tomás's end had come about was of no interest to Dorian. Such dramas lost their excitement the moment they were over. Perhaps the outcome had been inevitable, for what was left for the monk but to take his own life?

Dorian cast aside his memories of Brother Tomás, storing them away with those of Sibyl Vane and Basil Hallward and Celestine and Omar and the countless others whose lives he'd destroyed since the afternoon he had stood before his portrait and uttered that fateful wish. Although he had destroyed some of these lives by accident or for expediency's sake, the most recent had been deliberate and for the sheer pleasure of it. Dorian held the power of God in his hands—and he had no retribution to fear from having taken it.

Making his way to the coast, Dorian headed south, traveling along the lengthy perimeter of the South American continent until he'd circled around and reached the north at the other side. Along the way he passed through Chile, Argentina, Uruguay, and Brazil. Each country possessed its own unique flavor and charm—and each came amply supplied with its own vices for him to sample. The Dorian Gray who had believed himself to be pursued by the ghosts of his past had at last been freed by time and geography.

In Argentina Dorian's lust for the bodies of men continued, thanks to the prevalence of the *gaucho*. Often living outside the law, these strong and silent young men were fiercely proud and independent but prone to violence, their *facóns* always at the ready in their sashes should bloodletting be required. There was a romantic and dangerous quality to them as they rode atop their horses, herding cattle or sheep or simply passing through the towns and villages, their whips at their sides. That they were fully capable of using them without much provocation Dorian had no doubt—and his hunger for sensation inspired within his corrupt soul the desire to experience it firsthand. The thought of the leather striking his naked flesh gave rise to a need similar to that which he had experienced with Omar—a need for intensity and subjugation that was completely opposed to the role he'd played with Brother Tomás.

Dorian did not have to wait long before a suitable candidate crossed his path—a man whose ravaged countenance bore a hate so black he knew immediately that he'd found the perfect partner. Omar was a schoolgirl compared to this black-hearted brute, with his hard mouth and hard eyes. That he was hard where it typically mattered most became evident the moment they saw one another in a dusty saloon, though it was not what the fellow had in his trousers that Dorian wanted. The kind of man he sought would not condescend to deposit his seed inside another man's body. Instead he would seethe with hatred from his desire to do so, turning his whip against anyone who inspired such desires.

They discovered themselves seated next to each other at the bar, downing whiskey after whiskey as the setting sun turned red over the dry landscape. Dorian could smell the sweat of a long day's work on the *gaucho* and see the dirt filling the crinkles of his knuckles as his fingers brought the glass of golden liquid to his lips. There was a strength and cruelty in those large hands that excited him and made him want to become the recipient of it. Dorian paid for the whiskey, his only thanks the erection that mirrored his own.

There was no need to exchange names, much less the niceties of conversation. Leaving the bar, they walked along a dirt road until they came to a derelict old barn whose roof was partially caved in. Inside Dorian stripped off his garments, offering up his flawless body to the searing bite of the whip, his heart slamming inside his chest as he heard the leather hissing through the air before making contact. It sliced into his flesh like a knife through butter, sending his senses whirling and blood flowing. Bracing his palms against the splintered wall and planting his feet widely apart, he stood with his back facing outward, blindly awaiting the next strike, thrilling from never knowing where it might land. One moment his shoulder was struck, the next his buttocks. Sometimes it even dispatched a fiery lick in the fissure between them, which proved so excruciating he almost lost consciousness, yet still his fluids splashed against the barn wall as he came.

Each contact of the whip was a burning kiss of hatred—a hatred so pure and refined that Dorian was envious of it. It astonished him that someone could harbor an emotion so deep that it dripped from his pores like toxic oil. He'd never experienced hate in such a heightened form. To be the beneficiary of every drop of poison that flowed through the veins of this man gave rise to climaxes so extreme that Dorian felt as if he were falling off the edge of a cliff into a chasm that had no end. Whether the other man underwent a similar occurrence he didn't know, since no portion of his costume was ever removed and no sound passed through his lips.

Although it was never verbally arranged, they met several more times at the bar to drink whiskey and afterward visit the barn, where Dorian once again offered his naked flesh to the whip. As with all new sensations, their inevitable familiarity eventually bred boredom. The marks on his shoulders, back, thighs, and buttocks faded, as did his taste for flagellation.

Dorian next stopped for a while in Brazil, having heard many high tales about the country from other travelers he'd met along the way. Here he discovered a wealth of bordellos in which to reinvigorate his lust for the bodies of women. Having spent so much time with the hard bodies of men Dorian suddenly hungered for the soft sweet flesh belonging to the tender sex. He stayed in a coastal village that catered to passing seamen who had a similar desire for female flesh—a desire shared in equal measure with those for strong liquor and dangerous games of chance. These were not honorable seafarers who protected the country's waters or transported goods from one place to another. These were men who lived along the fringes of society, eking out a living from piracy on the high seas and money won from betting; they thought nothing of slitting the throat of a fellow gambler who could not afford to pay his debts.

With his deceptively guileless mien and abundance of cash, Dorian became part of their inner circle, exhilarated by the risks and the thrill of seeing which card determined who should live or die. He moved easily between the fragrance of women in the bordello to the stink of fear in the squalid gambling den on the village's rotting pier. The latter became an aphrodisiac as he drove the stakes higher and higher until he smelled the filth as those who couldn't pay soiled their trousers, knowing they would not be alive to see the next sunrise. Although an unpaid debt was of no consequence to a gentleman of means such as Dorian, he knew it was a matter of grave consequence to his companions at the card table; therefore he considered it his duty to join with them in collecting a life in return for what was owed, not minding in the least that he got his hands dirty in the process. He understood this kind of honor and enjoyed the simplicity of it: if one could not pay, one should not play. The foolish fellows who chose to gamble did so of their own free will, knowing that the outcome should they lose might prove fatal. To go from the pleasures of the boudoir to the pleasures of blood in the span of one night was an experience that would have inspired awe even in Lord Henry.

As Dorian sank deeper into the foul recesses of the cesspit in which he'd eagerly placed himself, he experienced a return of The Dream. So many years had passed since its original unveiling that he had forgotten all about it. Why it should recur when he had no demons to plague him made no sense. It was as though a breeze scented with honeysuckle had entered his room, blowing away the putrid stench of his life, leaving it fresh and clean and pure just as it had been before he'd been seduced by Lord Henry's hedonistic philosophies. When he awakened to find the cheap squalor that surrounded him, it felt as if someone had reached inside his chest and torn out his heart. Dorian tasted the sweetness of ripe cherries on his lips—kisses that had been placed upon them by the exquisite creature with the honey-colored eyes and hair who once again featured prominently in his sleeping world. What did she want from him?

Although he continued with his daily diet of frequenting brothels and the card table, the young woman came to him again and again in his sleep until he thought he would go mad from emotions of which he had believed himself no longer capable. To fall in love with a fantasy image was surely enough to get a man locked away in an asylum for the duration of his life—yet Dorian had no other word to describe what he felt. The scent of whores lost its appeal, as did the scent of spilled blood from the men upon whom Chance had turned. The ugliness of Dorian's life was now displayed in all its visceral filth by the beauty that haunted his sleep.

He could remain here no more.

NEW ORLEANS,
PRESENT DAY

Those who are faithful know only the pleasures of love: it is the faithless who know love's tragedies.

—Lord Henry Wotton

The dank smell of the river and the stink of the swamp mingled with the reek of garbage, stale beer, urine, vomit, and the sickly camouflage of deodorizer, the latter of which never quite succeeded in masking the odors the visitor's bureau preferred tourists not to know about. Such was Dorian's introduction to Bourbon Street in the city's French Quarter. For him it was the bouquet of opportunity rather than an insult to the nostrils. There was life here—life in all its dissolute glory, as swaying figures moved in a *corps de ballet* traveling from bar to bar, their celebratory cries and shouts an aria as painful to hear as it was exciting.

Decadence was in the air, and it had Dorian's name upon its lips.

From the moment he'd arrived in New Orleans he knew he had come home. There was a familiarity to the streets and bars and cafés and even in the clattering of the streetcars that moved along St. Charles Avenue. It was not a familiarity that brought boredom, but one that stimulated him and made him long for new experiences and new sensations. This decaying city called to him.

Dorian knew all about decay. His portrait had taught him its meaning. He wondered what the proprietors of the voodoo and occult shops would make of his portrait. The fact of its existence was far more frightening than any of the potions and hexes and other hocus-pocus they sold to gullible tourists seeking love or revenge or whatever they hoped to attain by drinking the contents of a glass vial or sticking pins into a wax figurine, but it had allowed him to roam like a nomad through the changing of three centuries. It was time to set down roots and embrace life with a fresh passion.

Dorian Gray had been reborn.

He spent his nights on the streets of the Quarter, learning their peculiarities as a blind person learns Braille until it had become second nature. Dorian came to know every crack in every sidewalk, every panhandler and drug dealer lurking in the shadows and beyond. He came to know the name of every spice that teased his nostrils and later, his palate as he parted happily with his newly acquired American dollars in the restaurants that beckoned him inside. He could taste the city's rich history in the line of every building and in every glass of liquor he consumed, for spirits both liquid and unearthly flowed harmoniously in New Orleans.

Dorian's beauty attracted the attention of everyone who saw him, but he spoke little except when absolutely necessary. Though lust was always present in his loins, he made no effort to assuage it. It was as if he were saving himself for something more exalted than a forgettable encounter inspired by a few cocktails in one of the French Quarter's many bars. In these drinking establishments women and men were available like street taxis with their roof-lights illuminated, fearless in making their desires known as they boldly made eye contact with anyone who caught their fancy. That Dorian was usually the recipient of their sexual attention was to be expected, yet he wanted none of it. Instead he returned to his hotel room alone, lying awake in bed until dawn tinted the window a watery yellow, *waiting.*

He would not need to wait for long.

Like a dog sniffing out a bitch in heat, Dorian located a group of single-minded spirits with a passion for sensation and a complete absence of morality. They too preferred to confine their activities to the night. That was when the shadows came to life, along with the revelers. It was a time for the dissolute to come out and play.

It was a time for the Night People.

In the beginning they reminded Dorian of himself back when he had balanced on the precarious ledge between his human self and the creature he'd been turned into by the utterance of a fanciful wish. As he came to know them better, he realized that for these appealing young people there was no ledge—they had taken the leap into the abyss of evil, where they wallowed joyously. Would they take it all back if they could? Probably not. Would he? He knew the answer to that as surely as he knew his own name.

The Night People dressed in sumptuous velvets trimmed with lace, elegant brocades, and sensuous silks that clung to their thin young bodies, making them look as if they'd stepped out of New Orleans's past rather than its present. Here the resemblance to a bygone era ended. They lined the upper and lower lids of their eyes with black, both the women and the men, which gave them an androgynous appearance. The kohl made them look even paler than they naturally were—a condition further emphasized by the whitish powder they applied to their faces and by the fact that they rarely ventured out into the sunlight. The makeup lent a touch of the exotic to countenances that were moderately attractive by making them strikingly so, though one member of the group would have been arresting even without any form of artifice.

Their beverage of choice was absinthe laced with cocaine, which they drank before setting off for the evening. It provided just the edge they required, heightening their senses and adding color to the nocturnal hours. If laziness got the better of them, they settled for port. They usually concluded the night with *café au lait* at their favorite outdoor café before returning home to sleep away the daylight hours. Dorian would discover that their lives consisted of many such rituals, most of which weren't nearly as mundane as the selection of liquid refreshment.

The first time Dorian saw them was at an open-air café on Decatur Street. He'd stopped in for a *café au lait* and decided to linger for a while to watch the chaotic late-night world of the French Quarter pass by. He enjoyed the circus-like atmosphere in this part of the city. It reminded him of his days in Paris, though its elegance and sophistication were markedly absent. Dorian had to keep reminding himself that time could not remain static for everyone. This was a new century in a new country. Indeed, the world had changed, though he wasn't convinced it had changed for the better.

Almost immediately he noticed the deathly pale yet eye-catching young man seated alone a couple of tables away. Even if he hadn't seen him, Dorian would have heard him, for he was tapping an impatient staccato beat against the tabletop with his large ruby ring. That he wore the ring on his right thumb seemed unusual, but Dorian had by now learned that the youth of today made it a point to be unusual. They didn't always succeed. As they strove to be unique and—if he had the correct term—"alternative," they often ended up much the same as one another. This was not the situation with the young man wearing the ring. On the contrary, his every affectation—and they *were* affectations of a sort—gave the impression of being entirely original, as if no one had ever thought to move in the same manner or speak in the same tone of voice. Dorian found himself mesmerized by the young man's long fingers as they pushed shoulder-length strands of black hair away from his face and tucked them behind his ear, bringing into exposure a profile that was a splendor to behold, with a perfectly straight nose and thick fringes of lashes that caressed his cheeks each time he blinked. And his lips! They formed the most delightfully voluptuous pout, which Dorian later discovered could turn cunning and vicious.

Signaling for a waitress, he ordered another *café au lait* so that he could remain there watching this captivating creature who seemed so otherworldly and, he realized, so very like himself. Had he found his twin in twenty-first century New Orleans? Dorian could not let the night end without learning who he was.

If the young man felt Dorian's eyes upon him, he gave no indication. The ruby continued to tap its rhythm like an acclerating metronome. As if in answer to his call, two young men and three young women with ink-black hair and ghostly white skin approached the table. Greetings were exchanged, followed by kisses—Dorian noted they were all placed upon the mouth regardless of gender *and* executed with lips parted. These were not the chaste kisses of mere casual acquaintances, but kisses brimming with intimacy and sensuality. He had even spied a brief mingling of tongues, and he felt himself harden in response as he imagined the young man's tongue slipping into his mouth and meeting his own.

As he listened to their animated voices, Dorian experienced a surprising pang of longing, suddenly feeling very much alone in the world. In truth, he'd been alone all his life, even when he had a wealth of companions to share his intellectual and fleshly pursuits. Indeed, he had known many lovers, yet connected with none. Perhaps the only time he hadn't felt alone were those moments he'd shared with Lord Henry—and they were so long ago as to be specks of dust upon his memory.

The party of young people was larger than their table could accommodate; they procured chairs from surrounding tables despite a scowl of disapproval from the waitress who had just delivered Dorian's second cup of coffee. Yet neither she nor anyone else employed there made a move to dissuade them. Dorian detected a shadow of fear clouding her eyes as she turned to go back inside, leaving them to do as they pleased. The newcomers drew their wrought-iron chairs close together until they had formed a constellation around the striking young man with the ruby ring, making it clear who in the group held the greatest importance in their private hierarchy. Dorian overheard one of the women referring to him in conversation as Patrice. He repeated it softly to himself. It tasted pleasing on his tongue, like sugared rosewater.

After some time had gone by, Patrice turned his head, meeting Dorian's inquisitive gaze full on. His expression indicated that he'd known all along he was being observed and had simply been amused by it. Rather than looking away from Dorian, he held the gaze, his lips quirking up in one corner. His eyes were the color of violets and they glowed with a strange inner light, reaching inside his observer, the touch knowing and familiar. It was as if the young man's fingers were probing Dorian's body—he could taste them in his mouth and feel them deep in his backside as they searched for the hidden switch that would send him into ecstasy. By now Dorian had grown painfully erect as the eye contact between them held far longer than customary. Then suddenly it was severed, leaving him to wonder if he'd imagined the entire episode.

Patrice held court at his table, demonstrating an air of authority and superiority that none of the others had and likely never would. Their eyes dutifully followed his graceful hand as he brought his cup of *café au lait* to his mouth to sip, then the movement of his lips as he took delicate bites from his *beignet*. When he spoke, they clung to every word as if each was a rare and precious pearl plucked from an oyster's shell. Of the fact that they adored and worshipped him there could be no doubt. Having enjoyed only a brief moment of his attention, Dorian understood how such regard could develop into reverence.

Despite his mien of youth, Patrice wore about him an air of world-weariness and intemperance, leading Dorian to believe that he was considerably older than his physical appearance indicated. This led Dorian to speculate whether this mysterious young man with the violet eyes shared something else with him besides an extraordinary beauty. Had he uttered his own fateful wish just as Dorian had done, trading his soul for everlasting youth and beauty? As for his companions, they behaved in an almost juvenile manner, confirming in Dorian's mind that Patrice was almost certainly their elder.

"Do join us."

The voice contained an Old World elegance; it took several moments for Dorian to realize that the object of his attention had just spoken to him. By now everyone at the table had turned toward him, their pale visages wearing varying degrees of friendly curiosity. The women were quite pretty, as were their male companions. Joining them didn't seem like an unpleasant way to pass the time.

No sooner did he rise from his chair than a vacant one was slotted in at Patrice's left. Taking his cup, Dorian sat down. Introductions were made—the young women consisting of Athenie, Juliette, and Marceline, the young men Valentin and Julien. Having gone from a party of six to seven there was no space to be found. Dorian's knees and arms were tightly compressed between Athenie and Patrice. He felt oddly comforted by the heat of their bodies, which burned through their garments and his, as if bare flesh pressed against bare flesh rather than cloth against cloth. An image flashed in Dorian's mind and he saw himself lying naked between them on a bed draped with red satin, galvanizing his erection until he could barely breathe. When his eyes met Patrice's, it felt as if the latter knew of Dorian's suffering and longed to relieve it. "We are pleased that you have chosen to join us," he said, his words taking on an additional meaning that their recipient could not yet comprehend.

Dorian dipped his head in acknowledgement. "The pleasure is all mine, I assure you."

Once again Patrice's mouth tilted upward in one corner to indicate that something had amused him. "Indeed, so shall it be," he replied in a mysterious tone. Slipping his hand under the table, he cupped the swelling in Dorian's lap, squeezing it meaningfully before letting down the zipper that was the only barrier protecting Dorian's rigid flesh from the outside world, freeing it from its prison of fabric.

Dorian nearly cried out in shock, though it was quickly tempered by delight as Patrice's slender fingers wrapped around his aching flesh. While the rest of the group chattered away oblivious to the drama unfolding beneath the table, Patrice massaged Dorian's prick with a clinical expertise, palming the crest repeatedly so that the sleeve of skin slid up and down until Dorian thought he would go mad with the need to come. Suddenly he tasted blood and realized he'd bitten through his lower lip. A fiery flush stained his face and neck and he closed his eyes, surrendering to the delicious torment of

Patrice's hand bringing him to a torturous climax that seemed to go on forever, flowing from a well that had been buried so deeply inside him that he wondered if it were even possible that some part of him still remained whose pleasure had not been tapped.

When it was over, Patrice leaned in to kiss Dorian on the lips, his mouth tasting of violets rather than the coffee he'd been drinking. He brought his froth-flecked fingertips up to his mouth and licked them like a cat licking cream from a bowl. When he kissed Dorian a second time the delicate taste of violets mingled with the more potent almond flavor of Dorian's seed as their tongues laced together in a kiss deeper and more intimate than any Dorian had ever experienced.

The following afternoon Dorian moved into Patrice's home in the French Quarter. He hadn't even needed to think about it, accepting the invitation while the imprint of the other man's fingers still marked his flesh. He fell easily into the rhythms of the house, finding life in New Orleans full of pleasure and ease. He felt like part of a family. For Dorian this was a new sensation and one he'd never imagined having any desire to experience, yet he very much enjoyed this sense of belonging. Even more so he enjoyed seeing Patrice every day. Just knowing they were together under the same roof at the same time sent a current of electricity humming through his body even when they weren't in sight of one another.

None of the Night People had any means of employment—or any inclination toward acquiring it. Dorian deduced that everyone was living off Patrice's patronage, since he apparently possessed sufficient wealth to accommodate them all in his spacious but crumbling home hidden behind wrought-iron gates and tangled foliage.

The house was of the style popular during a time when the inhabitants of New Orleans had demanded the kind of privacy it afforded. It had a certain decaying charm that fit this city built among swamps and the restless spirits of the dead. The walled courtyard was wreathed with withered vines of wisteria and bougainvillea, as well as a fountain that contained more dead foliage than water. What little water remained was primarily from rain and had turned a slimy green. Its condition seemed somehow fitting.

Patrice never discussed how he derived his income, and contributions to help maintain the household appeared to be nonexistent. Yet there was always a plenteous supply of absinthe and port on hand to drink, all manner of sensory-enhancing substances to ingest, and a refrigerator and pantry stocked with a variety of edibles, the latter of which arrived twice weekly in a delivery van that pulled up outside the wrought-iron gates. It was Athenie's job to sign for the boxes and she took great delight in the responsibility Patrice had bestowed upon her. Her enthusiasm for the task further emphasized her youth, giving her a mien of innocence that was misleading and very often fatal to those who didn't realize what she was capable of. That she charmed the fellow who drove the delivery truck was obvious; even from his upstairs window Dorian could see the bulge tenting the driver's trousers as she approached, giggling merrily when she spied the boxes overflowing with the liquor and food he'd just finished unloading. It was the older ones who took the most notice—men with daughters her age, or even granddaughters. There was something terribly sad, even laughable in the lascivious way they leered at her. It reminded Dorian of the childhood tale about Little Red Riding Hood and the wolf. As for little Athenie, she was perfectly aware of her effect on these men and used it to her advantage.

Every delivery day Dorian watched from the upstairs window of his room as Athenie's slender form went skipping gaily through the courtyard on up to the gates where the delivery man stood waiting with his clipboard and order form for her to sign, her hair billowing like a black cape behind her, looking to all the world like a young girl playing a game of hopscotch. But Athenie's games were far darker. She played them with Dorian when he looped the long strands of her hair around her neck like a rope while she was on her knees before him, her mouth working at his erect flesh with increasing intensity as he drew the ends of her hair tighter and tighter, her hands moving desperately beneath her skirt as he gradually choked off her breath. By the time he'd released his pleasure into her throat, Athenie's jade eyes would be protruding from their sockets, her face turning the red of freshly spilled blood as she experienced her own pleasure, whereupon Dorian released his grip on her hair. She fell backward onto the floor, gasping. Her expression was that of an angel as she gazed up at Dorian, her hands tucked between her thighs as if to protect her chastity. "I've never done that with anyone else," she finally said.

"You've never taken a man into your mouth before?" asked Dorian, certain he was being made the brunt of a joke.

"Oh, no, I do that all the time!" Athenie replied with a grin. "I mean letting someone...you know...*choke* me. I guess it's kind of kinky, huh?" She giggled the little-girl giggle that never failed to charm anyone in possession of a male sex organ. "Wow. You probably could've killed me if you'd wanted to!"

"Yes, I suppose I could have," agreed Dorian, wondering if she were perhaps more naïve than he gave her credit for. "Were you not concerned that I might lose control and do just that?"

"But that's what made it so exciting! Anyway, I trust you."

Dorian smiled wistfully. "You might not say that if you knew me better."

"I don't need to know you better. Patrice brought you here to live with us. That's all I need to know."

Although he was tempted to regale Athenie with tales of his numerous debaucheries, he suspected it wouldn't have made any difference in the opinion she'd already formed of him. "And what does Patrice have to say about me?" he queried, his pulse quickening as he waited for the answer, only to find himself disappointed by it.

"Nothing." Seeing Dorian's crestfallen face, she added, "But Patrice never says much of anything."

Even so, he felt like a fool for asking.

As Dorian learned more about his new housemates, he came to discover that they all had their own peculiar quirks. One afternoon, after enjoying another dark encounter with Athenie, he decided to ask Julien about her. Outgoing in nature, Julien demonstrated a proclivity for gossip that often sparked a good deal of eye-rolling from the others. Anything Dorian wanted to know he could surely find out from Julien, though his eventual goal was to unlock the mystery of Patrice.

He found Julien in his room. As usual, the door stood wide open, indicating that privacy was not required.

Julien seemed to be the only member of the household who never shut his door, preferring to make his every action, regardless of how private, a public affair. He lay unclothed on the bed, stretching his limbs like a cat, his eyes still fuzzy with sleep. Seeing Dorian in the doorway, he waved him inside. Although the display of his nudity gave the impression of being quite casual, Dorian suspected otherwise when Julien made no effort to hide his erection. The young man had removed the hair from his groin area, its absence going some way toward giving the impression that he was far more generously endowed than nature had intended. It was a clever trick, though not one Dorian would ever need to employ.

At the mention of the young woman's name, Julien's face lit up. "So you wish to know about our little Athenie? She's very skilled, is she not?"

Dorian felt himself being scrutinized as he nodded in agreement. "Very."

"And you have yet to see her in action!"

"How do you mean?"

Suddenly Julien looked as if he'd said too much. "Nothing, nothing. You'll find out soon enough."

Dorian decided to let this pass. Julien was probably inventing intrigues where none existed in order to pique his interest still further. "But what is her story?" he tried again.

"Oh, I see that you don't know!"

"Know *what*?" Julien's habit of dangling little pieces of bait in front of his nose taxed his patience and Dorian didn't bother to keep the irritation out of his tone.

"Our little Athenie is still a virgin!"

This was not the response Dorian had expected. The

Night People were creatures of the senses like himself—to imagine that one of them could still be in possession of her maidenhood was extraordinary.

"I see that you don't believe me!" Julien's flat belly undulated in a wave of hysterical laughter that traveled to his erect flesh, causing it to bob up and down as if it were nodding in agreement. "Dorian, the expression on your face is priceless!"

"But surely this is not possible."

"I have no reason to lie to you."

Dorian shook his head. "It's ridiculous. You must be mistaken."

"I agree it's ridiculous. But do you think because Athenie gobbles down your cock, that makes her quick to open her legs?"

Dorian conceded the point, though the hypocrisy in it was more difficult to accept. Perhaps his new friends were not as transparent as they wanted him to believe. Ever since he'd arrived they had been welcoming and open—almost excessively so—yet the more time he spent in their presence, the more secrets and mysteries he stumbled upon. He suspected the biggest secret of all was still to unfold.

Dorian had no wish to linger in Julien's room. He'd been given an answer of sorts and, although curious about the rationale behind it, preferred to learn it elsewhere. He would not have objected to an encounter with Julien, whose pose made it obvious he was eager for one. A bit overt for Dorian's taste, Julien nevertheless had considerable appeal and a pleasing lack of restraint when it came to sharing his body with others. Although not one to turn away from opportunity, something held Dorian back. And that something was Patrice.

The Night People's enigmatic leader had made no further overtures toward him since that evening at the café when he'd seduced him with his hand. It puzzled him as to why Patrice was keeping his distance. Had Dorian offended or displeased him? Something exceptional had passed between them that night, and Dorian had believed it would continue and develop into other pleasures and explorations, but ever since he'd moved into the house Patrice had regarded him in only the most neutral way—friendly, but not intimate. Indeed, intimacy appeared to be the province of the other members of the household, who freely sought out one another for physical pleasure. Of course Dorian had done likewise, seeing no reason not to. Did Patrice disapprove? Had he expected Dorian to stay separate from such fleshly frolicking and save himself for some higher good? From what he had seen, Patrice remained aloof when it came to engaging in physical relations with his followers. He took the role of observer rather than participant in their liberal sharing of bodies. Perhaps he preferred to partake of pleasure with his eyes, though Dorian suspected it was also a way to hold himself above the others and thus maintain authority.

Dorian wondered what would become of the group should something happen to Patrice. He knew they would never survive on their own—that was how strongly linked they were to him, as if they derived their blood from his veins and their breath from his lungs. The five young people worshipped Patrice like a god and would have likely given their lives for him if called upon to do so. That Dorian was beginning to feel this same sense of worship added to the fear that he was failing some test whose rules and outcome he did not understand, but whose successful outcome determined whether his relationship with Patrice would evolve into something more.

The café on Decatur Street where he'd first met the Night People had now become a regular part of Dorian's life. This was where he and his companions gathered in the moments before dawn, drinking their *café au laits* and nibbling their *beignets*, looking like just another group of young adults with a penchant for vintage clothing and curious makeup relaxing after a night in the bars. "Chilling out" was the term they used, though they looked anything *but* chilled with the strange fever burning in their eyes—a fever that indicated the presence of various substances, both lawful and unlawful, along with dark desires Dorian had yet to witness.

In New Orleans he enjoyed a freedom he had not experienced since Paris—a sense of careless abandon combined with a lack of concern for the mores and opinions of traditional society. There was no one here to cast a condemning glance in his direction or disseminate scandalous reports of his behavior. People were living their lives rather than observing the lives of others. Each day Dorian felt himself journeying closer to anarchy, yet he sensed there was more—that the group was holding something back from him that they didn't think he was ready to experience.

Drifting through life with no concern for the future, the Night People took what they wanted when they wanted it, discarding their toys after they were finished. Athenie, Juliette, Marceline, Valentin, and Julien seemed to be caught in a perpetual state of childhood with Patrice as their father figure, though discipline was rarely meted out. As Dorian began to discover, wicked behavior was encouraged and even rewarded. An extended kiss on the mouth, the flicking of a finger within the folds of the women, a hand encircling the erect flesh of the men—these were the prizes Patrice condescended to offer, yet he did not do so often. Such rewards had to be earned and, as a result, were highly sought after. This inspired a distorted kind of competitiveness as each of his children tried to please him by means of some outrageous act committed against a stranger.

The sultry heat of a predawn New Orleans hung over the seven at their café as night in the French Quarter drew to a close. Valentin and Julien were sharing the sordid tale of their encounter with an inebriated young man that had taken place in the men's toilets of a strip club on Bourbon Street. The two often went there, though their interest had little to do with the young women who made their livings sliding naked down poles with their legs opened wide; they preferred the drunken male tourists, who unwittingly provided their own special brand of entertainment.

Their victim had been out celebrating with his male friends, enjoying what was commonly referred to as his "last night of freedom" before he was to be married the next day. Each wore identical white T-shirts, the fronts inscribed with the words "Jerry's Stag Party" and an image of a woman's bare breasts. The man of the hour had been drinking heavily, undoubtedly inspired by the fact that the beers and cocktails were not being paid for by him. Urged on by his equally inebriated companions, he repeatedly tried to thrust a rolled-up twenty-dollar bill into the rear orifice of the young woman dancing on the low stage until the club manager finally intervened, threatening the party with eviction. Suitably chastised, Jerry decided to seek solace in a stall of the men's room, either not noticing or not caring that the lock on the door had broken off. This was where Valentin and Julien found him, hunched over a grimy toilet with his jeans and underpants around his ankles and his aggrieved manhood clutched in his fist, the flat cheeks of his rump greeting them as they urged open the door.

"He seemed to be having some difficulty," said Valentin, trying to look deadpan, but not succeeding. "So we thought we'd try to help."

"Yes," chimed Julien. "He was definitely in need of a Good Samaritan!"

A moment later Jerry found himself bent forward over the toilet bowl with his forehead resting against the tank as Valentin and Julien each took turns with his bared backside, the noisy sound of their bodies slapping together resounding in the squalid men's room and sending the next customer scurrying back out the door before he'd even had a chance to relieve himself. Neither Valentin nor Julien paused for breath until they'd both completed their pleasure inside Jerry, who followed suit courtesy of his enthusiastically pumping hand. They left as their calling card a rolled-up twenty dollar bill, which Valentin deposited into the soon-to-be former bachelor's plundered backside.

"Oh, my dears, you should've seen his face when he turned around and saw us there behind him!" cried Julien, his eyes spilling over with tears.

"I doubt he ever came so hard in his life!" added Valentin. "I wouldn't be surprised if the wedding gets called off."

The young women giggled with delight at the tale

and even Dorian found it difficult not to join the laughter. "Did you give him your phone number?" Juliette teased, her cheeks flushing pink beneath her death-white pallor.

"At least he has money to pay for the call!" added Marceline, grinning wolfishly.

Juliette gave her a matching grin. "Twenty dollars is too generous. I wouldn't have left more than ten! After all, he got something out of it too!"

Like a disapproving father, Patrice's voice returned to the table a more sober air. "It is possible that the gentleman had been seeking precisely what you gave him, rather than going to the altar unfulfilled."

"Are you sure you don't mean *unfilled*?" corrected Julien, his tears liquefying the black that lined his lower eyelids. Athenie, Juliette, and Marceline shrieked with laughter, attracting the attention of the few remaining denizens in the café and out on the street, who turned toward the group with interest as if they too wished to be made privy to the merriment. Dorian imagined how carefree they must seem—as indeed, they *were*. They looked like art students from one of the universities. Since he'd come to New Orleans he had seen a number of young people going about with sketchpads who had adopted a similar manner of dress and makeup. He had heard it described as "Goth."

Dorian decided to lend his own form of calm to the discussion, hoping it would endear him to Patrice's good graces. He was finding the situation between them intolerable and continued to search his mind for some memory of what he might have done wrong that had led to his falling out of favor. He was desperate for the touch of Patrice's hand massaging him toward ecstasy as it had done at this very same table. The abrupt cessation of intimacy between them was like being disemboweled with a dull knife. "Did you not say that this Jerry fellow chose the stall that had a broken lock?" he asked. "Why use this particular one if there were others more secure at his disposal? I have to agree with Patrice that it does seem rather calculated."

"You're right," said Valentin. "He was probably hoping someone would walk in on him and do exactly what we did, the dirty bastard! I bet if we go back in a week's time he'll be there, waiting for us!"

"Or waiting for someone else," added Julien with a playful wink.

Despite the jocular mood at the table, Patrice remained sober and unmoved. Finishing his coffee, he pushed back his wrought-iron chair and rose, indicating to his rowdy children that the night had reached an end. "The only way to get rid of a temptation is to yield to it," he said before turning to make his way out toward the street.

Dorian sat in his chair in stunned silence. It sounded as if Lord Henry had spoken using Patrice's tongue. Had Harry not uttered those same words to him all those years ago? He was certain of it! Suddenly he realized why being in Patrice's good favor was so important to him. It went beyond the fanatical adoration the others had. Patrice was the father figure for these five aimless young people just as Lord Henry had been for Dorian. He'd allowed the older man to teach him about life and shape his thoughts and opinions. Harry had been the only person to whom Dorian had ever deferred—which perhaps explained why he was experiencing something similar with Patrice. Yet there were far more similarities between the two men than the utterance of a few words—and they gave birth to a thought so fantastical he dared not allow himself to hope it could be true.

With each day that passed Dorian became convinced that Patrice was a creature like himself, remaining forever beautiful and young through some mysterious means that had come from a similar godless form of magic. Patrice had all the appearances of youth, but there was something behind the façade that indicated the presence of a very old soul—perhaps one even older than his own. It was present in his manner and the way in which he spoke. It was present in his posture, as if several centuries' worth of history had been carved into the bones of his spine, relaying tales of depravities far greater than anything Dorian had experienced. These qualities struck a chord of familiarity that resonated deep inside him, giving further credence to his belief.

Did a portrait exist displaying the evidence of every sin and act of corruption Patrice had ever committed? The idea of it sounded like Gypsy superstition in these modern times, but Dorian couldn't deny the truth that had been presented to him all those years ago in the old schoolroom at his London home. He needed to know if it were possible that another like him could be roaming the earth, free from succumbing to the decay of age and the inevitability of death. Had he found his father, his brother, his partner in life? To imagine for a moment that he could have a companion for eternity gave rise to a longing so potent Dorian felt debilitated by it. He had to learn the secret of Patrice's existence, even if broaching his suspicions branded him a madman.

Dorian found him seated by the window in the front parlor, drinking a glass of port. Patrice's violet eyes registered surprise at having his solitude intruded upon, though his face showed no displeasure on seeing who it was. "Please," he said, indicating with his hand the bottle sitting out on the liquor cabinet. "It is an excellent vintage."

Dorian discovered that his hands were shaking; he barely managed to fill his glass without spilling as he felt Patrice's hot gaze boring into his back. Yet when he turned quickly around to confront it, Patrice wasn't even looking in his direction. Claiming the chair next to him, Dorian organized his limbs into a pretense of relaxation, wondering how best to proceed. He was saved the trouble.

"You are settling in nicely here, Dorian. This pleases me."

"I am pleased to be here," he replied. "And I am grateful for your hospitality. I feel very much at home." Although Dorian had answered honestly, the sense that Patrice and the others were holding something back—some secret part of themselves—continued to plague him. He'd seen it in the clandestine smiles the group shared with each other—smiles that never quite seemed to include him.

Patrice nodded, but made no comment. The silence between them stretched until Dorian began to fear this would be the sole extent of their conversation. Patrice had never demonstrated a propensity toward idle chatter; he would not have been at ease in the London society of Dorian's past, where idle chatter was the *raison d'être*. "In fact, I believe that I have never in my life felt so much at home," he added, hoping this would inspire Patrice toward a more gregarious mood.

"Yes. I suspected as much."

"The man you see before you is greatly changed. For too long I have lived the life of a nomad."

Patrice nodded again, as if he understood the feeling and empathized. "Why do you not return to your native England?"

It was a question to which Dorian had no answer. Why not, indeed? Perhaps because Lord Henry was no longer there but for the remaining dust of his bones that had surely been buried in the Wotton family cemetery. A London without dear Harry in it was a London Dorian did not wish to know. "I fear London is much changed from the time of my youth."

"Ah, but you are still young, are you not? The memories of your boyhood must be as recent as yesterday's sunrise."

Did Patrice appear to be mocking him? "I am perhaps as young as yourself," countered Dorian, intending the statement to be provocative. He could feel his blood moving through the chambers of his heart as he waited for a reply. It would be some time before it arrived.

"Is there something you wish to ask of me?"

The door had been opened. It was now up to Dorian to pass through it.

Patrice rose from his chair, seeming to glide the short distance to the liquor cabinet, where he refilled his glass with more of the tawny liquid from the port bottle. He stood facing away from Dorian, the velvet of his jacket displaying the elegant V-shape his shoulders and back formed as they tapered to his waist, the garment flaring out slightly at his hips and buttocks. Were he to live another hundred lifetimes Dorian would not have tired of looking at him. He could only imagine the astonishing beauty that lay beneath the elegantly tailored garments. He felt a rush of blood to his groin as he wondered whether he would ever know of it, his mind wandering toward images of their humid bodies grinding together as a violent rain thundered overhead. He could smell the ozone in the air as he bore down on Patrice, taking him hard and without mercy. It felt like a glimpse into the future.

Returning to his chair, Patrice sipped his port with all the ease of a man untroubled. Dorian feared that the door to revelation had been closed. He'd allowed his thoughts to drift too long and now the moment was lost.

"You are not drinking your port, my friend. Is it not to your liking?"

Dorian glanced at the glass clutched in his hand, noting that he was, indeed, guilty of neglecting its contents. He swallowed the liquid in its entirety, relishing the velvety burn as it trickled down his throat. "It is very much to my liking," he responded, setting the empty glass onto the table at his side to prove his words. The light from the lamp created rainbows in the cut crystal and he saw a tiny fragment of violet among them. When he lifted his eyes, they were met by another violet.

The time for revelation had come.

In his eagerness to seek a connection between himself and another of his kind, Dorian had seriously miscalculated Patrice's willingness to share confidences. No sooner had he given voice to his theory than the other man's pupils widened with rage, the violet irises darkening to black. Patrice's hand shot forward across the space separating them, seizing Dorian by the neck and squeezing until Dorian felt his consciousness slipping away. "Do you think I cannot smell the stench of sin rotting your soul?" he roared, his normally temperate voice shaking the walls of the room and rattling the window pane behind them. "And you dare to ask about mine?"

There was surprising strength in that graceful hand—a strength otherworldly and malevolent. It was a strength that could just as easily caress a man to climax as kill him. Until he'd felt those fingers at his neck, Dorian had still believed there might be a chance he could be wrong about Patrice, but the promise of death choking off his breath told him that his suspicions were genuine. There was something at work here that was terrifying and unearthly. Although there was little in life Dorian feared, he knew with certainty that Patrice feared even less.

The killing was unexpected.

Dorian had been stunned the first time, though this gave way to a curious form of sexual excitement that was enhanced when he was offered his first taste of blood from a dying girl's thigh. She'd been dressed in the shameless uniform of the carelessly young—a blouse cut low to expose her breasts and a skirt cut high to expose the fact that she wandered the streets of the French Quarter without the modesty of underpants—a fact which became evident when she stumbled in her spike-heeled shoes and fell over to the sidewalk.

She'd come staggering out of a Bourbon Street bar with a plastic cocktail cup in hand, its contents sloshing onto her bare thighs. Mopping up the blue liquid with her fingers, she licked them dry before taking another gulp from the cup. She was alone, which sent a frisson of anticipation through the group. The violet of Patrice's eyes turned an impenetrable black as he observed her unsteady progress. Dorian felt a collective tautening of nerves from his companions, as if something of monumental proportions was about to occur.

They set off at a discreet distance, following her down Bourbon toward Bienville, where she veered right, heading away from the French Quarter and toward the direction of Saint Louis Cemetery Number One. She appeared to have no idea where she was going or that she was entering a part of the city where it was unwise for a young woman to wander alone in a compromised state. Dorian could hear her laughing and talking to herself. His heartbeat quickened as he tried to imagine what the Night People had in store for her, since she had now become their prey.

The warning at the cemetery's entrance was a prophecy.

> VISITORS ARE WELCOME BUT ENTER THESE PREMISES AT THEIR OWN RISK. NO SECURITY NOR GUARDS ARE PROVIDED AND THE NEW ORLEANS ARCHDIOCESAN CEMETERIES DISCLAIMS RESPONSIBILITY FOR THE PERSONAL SAFETY OF VISITORS AND THEIR PROPERTY.

It was over in minutes.

"And now, my friend, it is for *you* to finish what remains." Patrice's eyes glowed like beacons in the moonlight as they fixed on Dorian. They contained a challenge.

Dorian shivered and felt himself hardening as he looked at the barely conscious figure Patrice held in his arms. Her bare legs dangled like a rag doll's beneath her, the spike heels lost somewhere in the night. His initial shock had worn off quickly, replaced by a scholarly fascination as he observed each of his friends feeding—no, *gorging*—upon the life-giving fluid in her body, seemingly unembarrassed that he was standing there watching and listening to the sound of their sucking mouths. Dorian had at last entered the Night People's inner circle.

Strengthening his grip on the dying girl to keep her upright, Patrice raised up the hem of her skirt, bringing into exposure her hairless sex. It looked pale and vulnerable, disturbingly childlike, though there was something predatory about the glistening slash of reddish-pink that came into view as her legs fell open. The moonlight reflected off the dark liquid seeping from her punctured femoral artery, which Patrice had bitten open for the others.

Dorian knew what to do without needing to be told. He dropped down into a squat and fastened his lips to her inner thigh, tasting the salt-metal of blood. The first heady spurt onto his virgin tongue combined with the scent of her sex almost sent him reeling backward and he grabbed her upper thighs to steady himself. His thumb found its way inside the heated crease of her sex, moving in a rhythm that caused the girl to moan. Even as she lay dying in Patrice's embrace she wasn't immune to pleasure. Dorian slipped his thumb inside, the intrusion welcomed by a profound sigh that trilled down her body and vibrated against his thumb.

An erection pushed urgently against the front of his trousers. Had his hands not been engaged, he would have sought his own pleasure with his hand. Thrilling from the frail moans coming from above, Dorian dragged his lips away from the bubbling wound and fastened them onto her sex, his thumb digging deeper. Weakened though she was, he could feel the girl's finale building, as was his own. The taste of arterial blood combined with the taste of her arousal made an intoxicating cocktail. If he did not free himself from his trousers he would be in danger of ruining them.

As if sensing his predicament, Athenie wedged herself into the gap between his knees and undid his zipper. A moment later his prick was in her mouth. Her lips and tongue worked it with the expertise of the finest whore, returning to Dorian a flash of memory of another night—one that had been spent in a brothel in 1920s Paris, not at the moonlit gates of a cemetery in twenty-first-century New Orleans. Though it had been nearly a century since Celestine had tasted his flesh, he hadn't forgotten the luxurious feel of her lips.

The dying girl began to thrust her pelvis into Dorian's face in a feeble series of undulations that must have cost her dearly, for she had lost a good deal of blood to the seven thirsty mouths that had drunk from her. Her face already possessed the waxy pallor that indicated Death was whispering its welcome into her ear. Dorian's submerged thumb felt the clenching of her inner muscles as she came, only to experience a powerful roiling in his testicles as he did likewise. Athenie swallowed the results with shimmering eyes, gazing up at him in adoration. She dabbed her lips on a silk kerchief gallantly provided to her by Valentin, who leaned over to kiss her, stealing a taste of Dorian's pleasure.

Patrice released the girl, who slumped lifelessly to the ground. Her flavor lingered like a fine wine on Dorian's tongue, made all the sweeter when she'd died in his mouth. The Night People stepped over the corpse as if it were a pile of dead leaves and left it at the cemetery gate, where it became just another number in the city's daily body count. Returning to the house they shared, they slept away the daylight hours with the innocence of children, suffering no remorse for their sins.

But Dorian could not sleep. His senses were too energized. He paced in his room, moving from the bed to the window, then back to the bed again. He didn't know if he wanted to be alone or wake the entire household to share his jubilation with them. Had he really drunk the blood of a young woman and drained the life from her? It seemed reasonable to conclude that *he* had been the one to kill her, since he had been the last in the group to drink. All this time he had imagined he'd indulged in every form of depravity there was, only to discover he had missed the greatest of them all! Although taking life was not unknown to him, this kind of destruction went beyond the simple act of causing death. It was spiritual. At the cemetery Dorian had felt the burning touch of Lucifer's hand upon his shoulder and his fiery breath singeing the tiny hairs at his ear, encouraging, then praising him. Yet this was nothing in comparison to the pride he'd seen on Patrice's face after it was over.

No longer would the Night People hide their innermost souls from him. They were one and the same now.

The bloodlust reminded Dorian of his portrait. The group absorbed the lives of those they took just as his portrait absorbed the ugliness of his deeds, preserving him in perpetuity as a young man. Did drinking the life from others also prolong their existences?

He had heard of vampire folklore and knew there were actually people who enjoyed patterning themselves after these creatures as a means to achieve an unearthly sort of glamour. Witnessing the Night People on a kill made Dorian wonder if such legends should not be so easily dismissed. Was he not of a similar nature—and therefore likewise immortal through supernatural intervention? Yet perhaps the real truth to the legend was that they themselves believed in it.

Dorian found himself looking forward to the next spilling of blood, never knowing when it would come or whether their next victim might be male or female. The uncertainty fueled his excitement until he was as hard as granite. Although Patrice's followers would have been happy to go out into the city every night to hunt for a plaything, the killings needed to be staggered so as not to draw too much attention to their unusual nature. Those who were brought home instead of being killed on the street joined the ranks of missing persons not uncommon in a city such as New Orleans. After everyone had finished playing with the latest new toy, Patrice drove out into the country to deposit the body in the bayou, where it likely became a meal for an alligator. Dorian had to admire the genius of it; he was disappointed to learn that Patrice wasn't the first to conceive of such a convenient means of disposal. For generations the bayou had been a popular location for discarding unwanted bodies, which probably explained why much of the local gator population was grossly overweight.

The bars and nightclubs of the French Quarter provided an abundant supply of alcohol-saturated tourists and locals, the drink often prompting them to drop their guard. With so much fodder on offer, the

Night People could afford to be choosy, preferring to gorge on foolish young women who left all common sense behind upon entering the city—especially during Mardi Gras. The celebration became a smorgasbord of blood and sex. Young women crowded the streets of the Quarter, pulling up their blouses and T-shirts to bare their breasts in return for a tawdry string of beads to wear around their necks. It required little effort to separate them from friends and lovers with the promise of still more beads. Dorian would never have believed that an object as cheap and trivial as a string of beads could be used as bait, but it worked every time. The crowds of revelers would often become so wild it wasn't even necessary to lure a female victim to a quieter location. The bloodletting took place right where she stood, in full view of everyone, as Patrice's teeth tore through the flesh of her neck, starting off the rich flow of red that would nourish the entire group as they moved in to form a tight circle around their victim now that the real festivities had begun.

Occasionally they desired more of a challenge. They would then head for the Garden District, taking a streetcar and observing the comings and goings of the other passengers until they spied their next victim. Dorian's relationship with Patrice was still cooler than he desired. Their intimacy had never been repeated—a fact which went some way toward tarnishing his enjoyment. As they rode along St. Charles Avenue, he saw an opportunity to make himself worthy of Patrice's attention.

The young man was seated a couple of rows ahead, staring out through the rain-splattered window at the grand old homes lining the Avenue, their brightly lit windows offering an invitation that would never come to fruition for someone like him. He wore his wiry black hair in a multitude of tightly woven braids, the ends of which terminated in a small bead. He'd attracted Dorian's notice the moment he got on the streetcar; he had the youthful arrogance of one caught between boyhood and manhood. Back in the time of Basil Hallward, Dorian too, had been filled with this youthful arrogance—that all-encompassing sense that no one but himself was of significance. He could see the same characteristics just by the angle at which the young man held his head. Dorian wanted to strip it away until all that remained was the primordial nature of desire and death.

The youth got off at Canal Street, where he proceeded on foot in the direction of the interstate highway roaring noisily over the city. He walked with a self-assured swagger, as if seeking to challenge anyone who dared to cross his path. The Night People followed, led by Patrice, whose eyes had already begun to flicker between violet and black—an indication that something thrilling was about to happen. They were entering a neighborhood most chose to avoid unless they lived there, yet there was little the group feared, even if the color of their skin marked them as outsiders. The danger of their surroundings added to their mounting excitement, as did the fact that the young man with the braids exuded an air that indicated he would not be taken easily.

Like a lion pouncing on an antelope, Patrice brought him down in seconds.

They dragged the youth into a weed-infested parking lot that hadn't accommodated a car since before the last big hurricane. A bullet had rendered the only streetlight in the vicinity useless and the overcast sky made the lot even blacker. A colorful series of epithets sprang forth from the young man's lips, a number of which made reference to Patrice's mother as well as other female members of his family. Patrice merely laughed, catching in his palm an enraged fist while twisting his verbal offender's other arm painfully behind his back. Bringing his lips close to the young man's pierced ear, he hissed: "Tonight you shall die."

It was a perfect night for death. It was also a perfect night for Dorian to alter the pecking order.

The women clustered around the struggling figure as Patrice held him firm, their eagerness brightening their powdered white faces. "Please, can I go first?" begged Juliette. "I never get to go first!"

"It is not yet your time, little one," replied Patrice, his voice unusually tender. It sent a quiver of arousal through Dorian's body as he hardened with desire for this man who was perhaps as immortal and beautiful as himself. How much longer was Patrice going to make him wait?

"But when will it be time?" Juliette whined petulantly, looking about ready to stamp her foot on the ground.

"Temper, temper," warned Patrice, his tolerance for childish behavior clearly being tested.

"But—"

"Good things come to those who wait."

Dorian stepped forward. "And does that tired old proverb also apply to me?"

Patrice's eyes glittered with amusement. He held their victim's neck in a clench lock, his lips a hair's width from the pulsing snake of his jugular. Grabbing hold of the braids, he jerked the young man's head back so that the vulnerable flesh of his throat was bared. "Am I to understand that you wish to do the honors?"

"You understand correctly."

The air between them vibrated with a deadly energy. Dorian had cast down the gauntlet—it was up to Patrice to accept the duel.

Juliette's mouth opened as if she intended to lodge further protest, but a sharp look from Patrice silenced her. When he finally spoke, the amusement in his eyes had been replaced by approval as they met Dorian's. "Perhaps, my friend, you are ready."

"We must all lose our virginity when it is our time," said Athenie, her jade eyes gleaming with an unwholesome light that brimmed with memories of blood and death. Placing her hand on Dorian's arm, she patted it encouragingly. "It's an experience you will never forget!"

Dorian nodded in agreement as he remembered Athenie's first time, though the virginity to which she referred had nothing to do with a sexual deflowering.

Her girlishness had attracted the notice of many men, particularly those who might have been wiser to keep their sights set on women their own age rather than plucking ones not long out of the cradle. Athenie reveled in the salacious leers and suggestive comments they directed toward her, all of which she encouraged with her giggles and coquettish body language. She gave every indication that she would be following through on their indecent proposals, with no intention of offering her sweet young body for them to maul and salivate over. To her it was just a game, and she always emerged the winner.

For one man the game had turned deadly.

Athenie had found him in Jackson Square on a cloud-shrouded Sunday afternoon, looking for the most part like a typical tourist in his khaki shorts and T-shirt. He appeared particularly interested in a group of teenage girls who had just emerged from St. Louis Cathedral—he was surreptitiously catching them in the viewfinder of his camera each time he aimed the lens at the cathedral. It was obvious he was in New Orleans searching for a specific kind of mischief he couldn't find at home—and Athenie was more than happy to supply it.

Or so he'd believed when she approached him asking if he'd like for her to take his photo.

She allowed him to buy her a daiquiri at a nearby bar, and then another while he kept pace with double shots of bourbon. Neither of them had eaten and despite his hand repeatedly squeezing Athenie's bare thigh, he didn't seem inclined to offer to buy her dinner. Instead a third round of drinks materialized on the bar, followed by the man's thick fingers pressing into the gusset of Athenie's panties. The front of his khaki shorts pitched outward like a tent, and she giggled as he made copious references to what she might like to do with the contents, his fourth round of bourbon inspiring him to unzip his shorts so that she could slip her hand inside. Although she did so to humor him, Athenie was biding her time until dusk dusted the city in varying shades of gray. Then she made her move.

Her flirtatious conduct, followed by the promise of her mouth upon him, was more than sufficient to lure the fellow away from the busyness and relative safety of Jackson Square with its throngs of tourists and hawkers. Dorian and the others followed as Athenie led her prey out of the French Quarter, ignoring his repeated suggestions that they go back to his hotel for "some fun." It was obvious that he was getting anxious at the increasing shabbiness of the vacant streets and empty lots in a neighborhood that was not promoted in the city's tourist guides.

Silencing him with a kiss on the lips, Athenie grabbed his perspiring hand as he stumbled drunkenly after her, laughing like the carefree young girl she gave every appearance of being. As they approached an abandoned building, she paused to kiss him again before he could protest further. Broken glass and garbage littered the front, as did used hypodermic needles, their tips encrusted with blood. The windows of both floors had been smashed in and the main entrance door, which had at some point been removed, was covered over with boards, one of which swung loosely like the broken wing of a bird. The façade of the building had been embellished with a variety of painted symbols, slogans and drawings, the most colorful of which was of an oversized penis entering a woman's mouth. Here Athenie chose to stop.

The group likewise came to a stop, blending themselves into the shadows alongside another abandoned building across the street. They watched with varying expressions of amusement as Athenie placed her hand against the front of the man's shorts, rubbing with her palm until all talk of hotels had ceased. Giggling with delight, she undid the zipper, liberating the man's erect flesh. "Oh, my!" she cried, her eyes going unnaturally wide. "Is all that for me?"

The man chuckled obscenely. "Do you like it, baby?" he drawled, grabbing his prick and squeezing until it looked angry enough to burst.

"Oh, yes, I like it lots!" Athenie danced a girlish jig of excitement on the sidewalk, clearly enchanting her new playmate, for whom the dangers of the neighborhood and encroaching darkness had ceased to be of concern. Indeed, had a bomb gone off he wouldn't have forfeited the chance to live out his fantasy.

Placing his hand atop Athenie's head, he urged her down to the sidewalk, untroubled by the proximity of broken glass to her bare knees as she knelt before him. "Now open your mouth for Daddy!"

Athenie did as she was told, gazing up at him with an expression of such angelic innocence that she looked as if she belonged on a stained-glass church window rather than among the filthy detritus of the sidewalk. Grasping hold of her long black hair, he drove his pelvis into her face with impunity, his head lolling from side to side like a marionette with a broken neck as Athenie knelt in supplication before him, her hands clasped daintily behind her back.

The tourist's tormented groans eventually reached a homeless man sleeping in a nearby dumpster. A lice-ridden head popped up over the rim to investigate the cause of the disturbance. Seeing the activity transpiring a few feet away, he propped his bearded chin on the dumpster's ledge to better enjoy the show, unaware that the final act would be anything but a happy ending for the player in the starring role.

As the man's climax approached, Athenie allowed his prick to slip out from between her lips. Before he'd realized what had happened, she had dragged his shorts and underwear down to his oversized canvas shoes, trapping him as securely as if rope had been used to bind his ankles together. Although her mouth was still in the same vicinity, it had shifted away from the zone that most concerned him, locking instead on his inner thigh, where the little pearls of her teeth bit into his femoral artery. Blood spurted in every direction, mixing with the broken glass on the sidewalk like a cocktail poured over ice.

"Oh, shee-it!" came a voice from the dumpster. The lice-ridden head disappeared back inside, where it would remain until the performance had ended.

Athenie's first kill would not be the cleanest, but what it lacked in elegance it more than made up for in enthusiasm. Refastening her lips on the hemorrhaging wound, she wrapped her arms around the man's buttocks to hold him firmly against her face, slurping noisily on the opened artery. Although petite, she was far stronger than she looked. His neglected manhood shriveled up into a sad facsimile of itself, his seed spilling onto the sidewalk. Shock coupled with the fact that he'd drunk so much bourbon made his struggle ineffective. His hands flapped impotently at his sides while his mouth emitted a sort of keening warble that grew fainter the longer Athenie sucked on his thigh.

She might have drunk him dry had the others not gone over to join her for their share of the spoils. When they had finished, they dragged the man's lifeless body over to the wall of the empty building and propped it up into a sitting position directly beneath the fellatio-themed painting, where he remained until someone finally called the police—but not before his wallet had been removed from the pocket of his blood-stained khaki shorts.

For the entire week following the event Julien sounded the baritone refrain of "Open your mouth for Daddy!," sending the group into peals of adolescent laughter. Dorian had even caught a tiny smile on Patrice's lips, giving him a charming boyishness that made Dorian more determined than ever to taste that violet-flavored mouth again and thrill to those skillful fingers on his naked flesh.

Indeed, the cocksure young man from the streetcar seemed like the perfect opportunity for Dorian to establish a more intimate bond with the Night People's leader.

Patrice continued to enclose the youth's neck in an iron grip as he hovered between consciousness and oblivion, the reduction of oxygen to his lungs making any fight ineffective. The dark braids formed a curtain for his face; his head hung over the crook of Patrice's arm as if he were already dead. Patrice's eyes locked into Dorian's as if daring him to follow through. They stood staring each other down as the others backed away in deference. Without warning, Patrice flung him at Dorian. "He is yours."

Dorian caught the young man in his arms before he could regain enough of his wits to flee. Replicating Patrice's neck lock, he pulled his victim close so that the artery pulsing beneath the thin layer of skin on his neck was located at his lips. He could hear the blood flowing through it, giving life to the body whose life the group intended to take. Although he'd drunk from the arteries of their victims before, Dorian had never actually opened one with his teeth. The accelerated beating of the young man's heart was like a hammer pounding in his ears and he felt the fullness of the erection inside his trousers, knowing it was visible to the others.

By now everyone's eyes were on him, though there

was only one set that mattered. Their violet light seemed to caress him, probing like a physical entity, pushing deep until it felt as if he'd been filled by another man's hard flesh. It was similar to what he'd experienced when Patrice's hand had brought him to pleasure at the café—an invasion of the body, but one that was very much welcomed. At that moment Dorian truly did feel immortal.

The young man's fear was a potent bouquet as Dorian's teeth broke through the tender skin of his neck. He felt a tiny snap as the artery burst open. The first rush of hot coppery liquid into his mouth was enough to trigger a preliminary rush in his trousers as he sucked at the wound he'd torn into his victim's neck. For a moment everything went black. There was no sight, no sound, no movement, no smell—just an infinite nothingness that lasted for he knew not how long until he was finally returned to his body. An overwhelming wave of sensation slammed into him, nearly knocking him off his feet. He heard a scream and thought it had come from the young man he held in his grip, only to realize it had come from himself.

Dorian was startled by the gentle touch of a hand upon his shoulder. "You have done well, my friend," said Patrice. "But it is time to share your prize." Taking the drooping body from his arms, Patrice placed his lips at the same location, drinking the bubbling crimson river, his eyes lifting to meet Dorian's, who saw in them an acceptance and a heat that had not been there earlier. It contained the promise of pleasures that would be shared exclusively between them.

After Patrice had finished, he held their victim steady so that the others could take their turn. Tonight it would be Julien who got to taste the final pleasure before death arrived to claim another life. He dropped eagerly to his knees, easing open the young man's jeans to perform upon him. Dorian wondered if the men and women whose lives they took realized that they would never again experience the wondrous act of climax, unconsciously triggering a response in their bodies that provided them with a physical ecstasy made more extreme by the nature of its finality. If so, he envied them for a sensation he was likely never to know. Indeed, was it even possible for him to die?

Dorian's thoughts were interrupted by a tortured moan as their victim's pelvis reared hard against Julien's face, each thrust brutal in its desperation since one of them would be his last. A moment later he was still.

Patrice released the lifeless figure from his arms. It fell to the cracked concrete in a heap of flesh and bone, making barely a sound, as if draining the blood and semen from it had also drained away most of its weight. Julien brushed off the knees of his velvet trousers, plucking from the nap a few errant bits of gravel, his face glowing beneath his pallor. Valentin ran over to embrace him, their lips joining in a lengthy kiss calculated to allow him a taste of their victim's final pleasure. They clung to each other like a pair of lovers reuniting after a lengthy absence, making it evident to everyone that they'd be sharing a bed when they got home.

The Night People made their way back to the French Quarter without incident. They passed a number of dubious-looking characters, but no one made any attempt to disturb, harass, or detain them. Although Dorian was fairly certain the killing had not been witnessed, the disinclination of the local drug dealers, thieves, prostitutes, gang members, and panhandlers to disturb them indicated that they sensed something was slightly off about the group.

The seven assembled at their favorite outdoor café, where they relaxed with their cups of *café au lait* and *beignets*, their faces flushed and their bodies overheated from the excitement of the evening. Dorian sat next to Patrice. It seemed like so long ago when they had met—he had entered the lives of the group as a stranger only to be accepted as one of the family. Tonight he'd sensed a definite shift in Patrice's manner toward him, like a block of ice that had finally begun to thaw. The fact that he had arranged it so that Dorian was seated by his side indicated that something had definitely changed between them.

Athenie, Juliette, and Marceline chatted happily among themselves, with Valentin and Julien joining in whenever the mood suited them, though it was obvious that tonight they only had eyes for each other. Patrice spoke little, and Dorian also found himself disinclined to join the conversation. The events of the night were catching up with him, along with the magnitude of what he'd done.

As if reading his thoughts, Patrice said: "You were most impressive this evening."

Dorian felt his heart skip a beat as he turned toward the other man. The violet of Patrice's eyes burned with a heat so searing it set fire to his loins and he flinched in embarrassment when he heard a groan of lust escaping from his lips. He felt like an awkward schoolboy who didn't possess the sophistication or skill to conceal his physical desires before they were ready to be welcomed by the one to whom they were directed. He nodded, not trusting himself to do more.

"In fact, you did superbly, my friend."

Drawing in a deep breath to steady himself, Dorian's voice came out barely above a whisper. "Thank you, Patrice."

Patrice paused to take a bite from his *beignet*, the movement of his lips conjuring up scenarios in Dorian's mind that he hoped couldn't be seen on his face. "Perhaps I have been too harsh," continued Patrice. "You may have noticed that I have not been as amiable toward you since the last time we spoke privately."

"Yes, I have noticed. And I have been trying to determine why."

Patrice's eyebrows formed a question. "And what conclusion did you reach?"

"I reached no conclusion at all."

"Indeed."

"And this is all you have to say on the subject?"

"What would you like for me to say?"

The mockery in Patrice's tone made Dorian angry enough to lash out with violence, yet it also inflamed his desires. There was something so damnably familiar to their banter. Had he not done a similar thing with Omar each time he wished to fuel his rage and, in turn, his passions? In playing with words, gestures and meaning, Dorian had played on Omar's predilection for brutality until it was directed back at him in the form of sex. Was Patrice playing the same game? "I would like for you to speak frankly," Dorian finally replied.

"I always speak frankly."

"And yet you say nothing."

Patrice sighed dramatically. "Then perhaps you are not really listening."

Dorian saw flashes of red at the corners of his eyes and realized he was clenching his teeth—the same teeth that had torn though the flesh of a young man's neck, opening him up to Death. Suddenly he felt a hand working in his lap. It was followed by the shock of the night air against his erect flesh.

"You shall come to my bed tonight."

The statement was a whisper of breath against Dorian's ear and he wondered if he'd imagined it.

Patrice gripped him firmly, squeezing and releasing until Dorian thought he would go mad with frustration. He had waited so long to feel the other man's touch on him again, only to end up tortured by it. That Patrice's intention was to simultaneously vex and pleasure him made the fury seething within him taste both bitter and sweet. Rather than bringing Dorian to climax, Patrice took him to the brink, then abruptly abandoned him there.

Reclaiming his hand, Patrice relocated it to his partially eaten *beignet*, which he finished off in two elegant bites, following it with the rest of his *café au lait*. Setting the empty cup carefully back in its saucer, he dabbed his lips with the paper napkin, refolding it into a neat square. He nodded toward the group, signaling that it was time to leave, ignoring the grumbles and whines of those who hadn't yet finished their refreshments.

Dorian knew he was being toyed with. Rage, lust, and indignation warred within him; he felt his control snapping like a string that had been pulled too tightly. He wanted to rip out Patrice's throat and drink him dry as he plundered him from behind, not stopping until the last breath had been expelled from his lungs. That he might conceivably do so was not beyond the bounds of reality. Never in his life had he been this provoked!

Despite Patrice's impatience to leave the café, he did not behave like a man in any particular hurry to return home. Instead he strolled through the Quarter like a poet in search of inspiration, as if he were in a garden taking in the fragrant blooms on a fine spring day rather than on a city sidewalk in the dead of night where the fragrances were those of a less pleasing nature. A pile of dung sat steaming in the middle of the street, deposited by one of the horse-drawn carriages that shuttled tourists about. When combined with the smell of frying fat from the restaurants, it formed a potent bouquet that was difficult to flush from the nostrils.

A five-minute walk ended up taking an hour, and the group was visibly relieved to finally be home. Normally they assembled in the parlor for their drink of choice before retiring, but not tonight. Everyone seemed to want to get on with their private agendas as quickly as possible. The front door hadn't even slammed shut before Athenie, Juliette, and Marceline went clomping up the stairs in their clumsy black boots followed by Valentin and Julien, leaving Patrice to do the locking up. As he dealt with the business of entering the burglar alarm code, Dorian stood fuming on the bottom rung of the staircase, silently daring him to retract the invitation to his bed. Without a word, Patrice took his hand and led him up the stairs.

There was an underlying odor of damp and decay in the bedroom that tarnished the richness of the silk and brocade furnishings and bedding. Dorian imagined that this was how the grave would smell, though he didn't find it disagreeable. On the contrary, it was a smell with which he should have been intimately acquainted by now. He watched as Patrice sat on a padded bench at the foot of the bed and began to undress, performing the function as excruciatingly slowly as he had his whimsical amble home. The boots came first, each metal buckle a mission in itself as his slender fingers worked them open. Placing them underneath the bench, Patrice pulled the socks off his well-formed feet, rolling them into two black balls and setting them on the floor alongside the boots, all the while pointedly ignoring his guest. Suddenly he stood up, stretching leisurely as if he were alone in the room rather than in the process of disrobing in the presence of another man—particularly a man who had come here solely for the purpose of having sex.

Dorian knew that Patrice's every action had meaning behind it, yet he remained where he was, waiting to see what would happen next. He was determined not to give Patrice the satisfaction of watching him lose control, though he wondered how long it would be before he finally did. His thoughts and emotions were in a turmoil from the long famine he'd been forced to endure. Now that his passions were so close to fruition, Dorian found them very much changed.

Patrice's fingers carefully unhooked the ornamental braiding that fastened together the front of his black velvet blazer. Slipping off the garment, he folded it and placed it neatly on the bench, then did likewise with the matching trousers, though there was a studied pause before he eventually stepped out of them—a pause Dorian knew was meant to inflame him, for the only article of clothing that remained to be removed was a white silk shirt, the front portion of which shielded a substantial erection, its imprint against the delicate fabric indicating that he wore nothing else.

The crown of Patrice's prick peered out from between two buttons on the placket, its flesh the same shade of pink as the roses in Lord Henry's garden at his home on Curzon Street. Why Dorian should form such a curious connection was incomprehensible, yet it had been the first thing that came to mind. He remembered the velvety softness of the petals as he rubbed them between his thumb and forefinger and cursed himself for wanting to discover if what he saw before him felt the same. How the sight of Patrice's arousal enraged him! Though this would be nothing compared to the rage Dorian experienced when the last garment was shed and Patrice stood naked before him, revealing a body as beautiful and perfect as his own.

"Do you intend to stand there all night?" The violet of Patrice's eyes taunted him, the object rising up against his belly doing likewise. It triggered a loathing inside Dorian so intense that he felt the room lurch sideways. Yet perhaps it was himself he loathed for his yearning to go to his knees and demonstrate which of them was more willing to capitulate to the other. Only a few weeks ago he would have been eager to do so, but tonight he refused to prostrate himself like a humble worshipper at the altar.

Dorian launched himself at Patrice, bringing him facedown onto the bed. Climbing on top of him, he straddled his thighs, trapping him beneath his weight. He'd had enough of being toyed with. Reaching down, he freed himself, his flesh aching with the need to ravage and plunder. Patrice's naked buttocks goaded him with their muscular perfection and Dorian pulled them savagely apart to expose the tidy little opening between them, wanting to incite shame rather than arousal. Instead it seemed to mock him, as if daring him to make use of it. Yet why should he find scorn when he had been granted an invitation?

Dorian felt the ghost of Omar at his side as he spat and took aim, determined to silence the mocking mouth and prove which of the two men in the room was the superior in this game of power. Whether Patrice's resulting cry was one of pain or pleasure he didn't know, nor did he care. Grabbing hold of his wrists, Dorian pinned them wide to the mattress, the element of crucifixion in the pose conjuring up long-ago images of Brother Tomás's tormented piety. Those had been moments of true power, when he had felt elevated to the level of a god. He wanted this again *now* as he hammered his way in and out of Patrice.

So caught up had Dorian become on reaching this higher plane of existence that he didn't even realize he had reached a climax before he was already laboring toward another, his ceaseless battering continuing until dawn began to tint the city with a lemon-yellow light. When his testes were finally empty, Dorian extricated himself and climbed off, confident that he had won the battle. He had shown no mercy; indeed, Patrice was lucky to be alive, for there had been a moment when Dorian had envisioned his hands encircling his neck and choking the life from him. It had seemed so real that his fingers could actually feel the bones crushing beneath them.

Patrice rolled over onto his back. The results of his pleasure lathered his belly and chest like soap. To Dorian's horror, he was still erect. Patrice smiled up at him, his violet eyes gleaming with satisfaction. "Once again you have exceeded my expectations," he said. "I look forward to sharing many nights of passion with you."

Dorian had expected to be verbally excoriated and perhaps even ordered to pack his things and leave the house. Instead he was being complimented for his performance. Rather than being the one who did the using, it was *he* who had been used. In trying to exert his supremacy, he had allowed himself to become a pawn in Patrice's game just as Omar had become a pawn in his.

He had been played for a fool by a man cleverer and more evil than himself.

The Dream returned.

More than half a century had passed since Dorian had been haunted by that beautiful face and those cherry lips that seemed to smile only for him. This was not the face of a woman he would cherish—it was the face of a woman he would defile. He'd made it his life's work to sully the pure and the innocent, corrupting them until they savored the filth in which they frolicked. With this young woman it would have been no different. Dorian would have devoted himself to her personal ruin, savoring every delicious moment of it. But no longer. He knew that if she were real, he would be so incapable of destroying her purity or allowing anyone else to that he'd have been willing to give up his life to protect her.

The thought troubled him. It made him feel vulnerable, impotent. At times it even frightened him. It hung over Dorian like a dank mist over the bayou—and it had all begun with the night he'd spent in Patrice's bed. Since then Dorian had gone out of his way to avoid him—or avoid him as much as it was possible to do, waiting for the summons he knew would eventually come, yet daring to hope that it wouldn't.

Perhaps he should have left. The home he believed he'd found no longer felt like home. The pleasure had gone out of the kill. Although Dorian loved New Orleans, he no longer loved his life with the Night People. He felt hollow inside, as if he were going through the motions rather than living the sensations. But something seemed to be holding him here, forcing him to stay.

And then he saw her.

Dorian did not believe in such things as presentiments, yet there she was, walking along Decatur Street late at night. *Alone.* She gave every indication that she knew where she was going, her faculties seemingly unimpaired by the copious amounts of drink or drug to be found. The city was rife with hooded young boys and men hawking the latest substances to smoke, swallow, sniff or inject. Even the Night People indulged on occasion, believing nothing could ever harm them.

As she made her way toward the less populated streets, Dorian concluded that she lived in the area and was going home after working in one of the bars or restaurants in the Quarter, or else she was a tourist returning to a cheaper and less favorably located hotel after a night out. Tourists on a budget made excellent targets, their choices of accommodation not always being in the safest parts of town, despite their advertised "proximity" to the French Quarter.

Patrice had been the one who spotted her, his eyes flickering between violet and black as they always did each time a prospective victim crossed their path. They had been on their way to their favorite café, not planning to indulge in anything more exhilarating than a *café au lait* and *beignet,* when the young woman rounded the corner ahead of them. Patrice's back and shoulders went rigid beneath his velvet jacket like a cat readying itself to attack. "She is ours."

He didn't need to say anything further—the Night People understood what was required of them.

They followed several paces behind, their excitement crackling like electricity in the humid air as the young woman's shoes clicked noisily against the cracked pavement. Dorian watched her long hair sweeping in a graceful arc across her back, turning a lush golden brown as she passed under a streetlamp. He was surprised to discover himself sprinting ahead of the others, including Patrice, whose angry glare he ignored. This creature being swallowed up by the dangerous night of the city intrigued him, and he had not even seen her face!

Having by this time left the French Quarter, the group began to close in. Here the streets were less populated, less lighted, less affluent. This was not an area where a woman's cry for help would attract chivalrous rescuers or Good Samaritans. If anything, it would attract still more predators to victimize her in the event there was anything remaining after the original perpetrators had completed their task. When the thick rubber sole of Patrice's boot crunched over some broken glass from a liquor bottle, she whirled around, her eyes going wide with terror as she saw the four men and three women who looked like the cast of a vampire film descending on her.

Dorian knew those eyes. They were the eyes from The Dream.

She took off in an awkward run, stumbling on the uneven pavement as she headed deeper into the darkness of New Orleans's no-go zone. Had she not panicked, she might have realized that she was sealing her fate by doing exactly what her pursuers wished her to, leading them to a location where they could subdue her without difficulty or threat of interruption.

Patrice reached her first, grabbing her up in one arm as if she weighed no more than a bird. He laughed cruelly as she tried to fight him, silencing her shriek with the palm of his hand. Her legs kicked and flailed in every direction, sending one of her shoes flying into the street. Liquid trickled down her leg as she wet herself in fear.

"She's a spirited one, isn't she?" Julien remarked in amusement.

"Maybe a bit *too* spirited," rejoined Valentin.

Patrice pinched his thumb and index finger into the nerves at the base of her neck, increasing the pressure until the pain had become so intolerable that she stopped struggling and went limp in his arms. As he dipped his head into her neck in preparation to bite, Dorian heard someone shout out: "No!" He was stunned when he realized it had been him.

Patrice's lips froze before the young woman's pulsing artery. He looked up at Dorian with dilated pupils, the irises now completely black. The others had gathered around, impatient for the fun to begin. "*No?*" he echoed. "What is this 'no'?"

Dorian knew that he needed to stop this from happening, and all he had to rely on was his wits and his fists against those of six other people, one of whom had already demonstrated that he could outwit him. "I just think—"

"You just think *what*?"

"—that maybe we should..."

"Come *on*!" wailed Athenie. "I'm thirsty!"

"Let's just get this over with. I'm tired," said Valentin, clearly unaffected by the physical charms of their victim.

"Oh, Christ, she's peed on herself!" cried Marceline. "I'm sure as hell not going down on her."

"I'm sure she'll survive without your talents, dear," replied Julien with a smirk. "Or maybe 'survive' isn't the right word."

"I think I'm beginning to understand." The smile Patrice gave Dorian was part disdain and part annoyance. "Am I correct that you wish to perform the deed yourself?"

The women bounced from foot to foot like children kept waiting too long for their treat. Dorian could hear Marceline's childish whining coming from somewhere behind him while Valentin and Julien grumbled to each other like a pair of cantankerous old ladies. Juliette stood with her hands perched on her hips, her pretty features twisting into a scowl of irritation that barely concealed her tears. There had been discord among the group since their last victim. Everyone had sympathized with Juliette, who, by rights, should have been the one to commence the bloodletting, not Dorian. The fact that he'd been allowed to go in her stead did not sit especially well with any of them. He was still in their eyes a newcomer and therefore last in line. Juliette was the only one in the group who had not been given her opportunity. But it was for Patrice to decide who went first and who didn't. And no one ever challenged Patrice.

Until now.

Patrice's smile turned venomous as he continued to stare Dorian down with Stygian eyes. "Are you becoming greedy, my friend?"

Dorian's heart felt as if it would hammer a hole through his chest. In moments the young woman Patrice held trapped in his arm would be dead. He was her only chance at survival, yet he couldn't understand why this responsibility had suddenly fallen to him. "*I* want her," he said. He knew the price to be paid for her reprieve would be high—and he was prepared to pay it.

Patrice made a tutting sound with his tongue, his grip on their victim loosening enough to offer Dorian hope. "I see you have developed quite a taste for our little pleasures. But what makes you think I would be willing to give her to you? Am I not to be allowed my little pleasures as well? It has been some time since I performed the deflowering—and I am hungry for it!" Patrice made as if he were about to bite into the young woman's neck, pausing to gauge Dorian's reaction.

Dorian kept his features impassive. He knew he was being goaded, but if he didn't handle the situation cleverly, the woman from The Dream would feel the life drain from her body. He needed to preserve the truce between them—and that meant doing anything he could to prevent Patrice from knowing his reasons for sparing the young woman's life—though, in truth, not even Dorian knew the reasons.

"And what will I get in return should I decide to give her to you?"

"Anything you want," replied Dorian, sickened by what he was offering. Their recent encounter had been enough for a lifetime—the thought of a command performance made him question whether the life of some woman was enough compensation for the payment Patrice would extract from him.

"But what about me?" protested Juliette. "When will it be my turn? It isn't fair!" She swiped at her streaming eyes, leaving sooty smudges of black on her white cheeks.

"Shut up, you stupid child!" shouted Patrice, his smile evaporating. "I shall decide whose turn it is or isn't!" His eyes bored into Dorian as if they could see into the rotted detritus of his soul. "You wish to be the first to open her?"

On hearing this, the young woman let out a terrific screech and resumed her struggle, no doubt envisioning unspeakable violations of her body by the four men and three women that surrounded her. Patrice clamped his hand over her mouth and nose until her lungs became starved of oxygen. She slumped forward in his arms, accepting the inevitable. Dorian had seen the human capacity to fight for life many times. Yet he had also seen its converse when realization finally dawned, revealing that there was no way to win. Seeing it again with this lovely creature from his unconscious tore at emotions he thought he no longer had.

Suddenly Patrice let her drop from his arms. Her head hit the buckling concrete with a painful-sounding thud. She lay there stunned, her body folding itself into a fetal position as if this might shield her from her assailants. In the tarnished glow from the only functioning streetlight that hadn't been shot out or had its copper wiring stolen, Dorian noticed the wisp of fabric beneath her skirt protecting her modesty. His instinct was to tear the pathetic little scrap from her hips and take her in full view of everyone, afterward joining with his companions as they drank her lifeblood until nothing remained but an empty shell of female flesh.

Her final pleasure was one he would have fought hard for the privilege of tasting.

Dorian felt his erection pushing against the front of his trousers and was deeply ashamed. One moment he wanted to shield her as if she were something precious to his heart, the next he wanted to debase her until not a breath emerged from her unsullied. Although prettier than most, she was just another young woman like so many others. Why should her life be of concern to him? Yet it was.

"Are you not going to begin?" Patrice was staring at him curiously. Juliette had ceased her whimpering and now stood at his side as if all had been forgiven. She, like the others, knew that it was wiser to curry his favor than to stand against him.

Dropping onto his haunches, Dorian gathered the young woman into his arms and stood up, draping her over one shoulder like a shawl. Patrice began to laugh, all traces of his earlier animosity gone. "So you wish to start collecting souvenirs?" The rest of the group joined in the laughter, the tension among them broken. Even Dorian found himself laughing, though he had no idea why. Unlike the others, his laughter would be short-lived.

"Very well. Then I suppose nothing remains but for us to take her home—" said Patrice, "—where we will make her our plaything!"

The whoops and cheers from the group tore through the New Orleans night, echoing in the bleak emptiness of the dying neighborhood. They were the cries of wild beings with no morality or fear. Before Dorian realized what was happening, Patrice had reclaimed the semi-conscious figure from him. Flinging it over one shoulder, he ran off into the night, the others taking off after them in excited pursuit as if they were participating in a children's playground game. Dorian had seen the young woman lift her head briefly to look back at him with frightened eyes. Then she was gone.

Racing to catch up, Dorian cursed himself for allowing Patrice to take him by surprise. For all he knew they were already feeding on her and all he'd accomplished was to earn her a few minutes' reprieve, rather than days or weeks. Yet what had he expected—that they would allow her to go free? The Night People were as merciless and greedy for sensation as he was. It had been foolish to think they wouldn't kill her. Whether it happened tonight or tomorrow or the next day was of no consequence. But happen it would.

By the time everyone returned to the house, daybreak was sliding onto the horizon. Although the group indicated a willingness to enjoy their new toy in the daylight hours, Patrice had other plans. "There will be plenty of time for pleasure later," he reassured his impatient followers. "For now, let us retire to our rooms for sleep. We will assemble in the parlor this afternoon to discuss what we have arranged for our guest. She will, of course, be present to hear our ideas and, I hope, to indicate which of them are the most repugnant to her." Patrice looked at Dorian with a sadistic gleam in his eyes that sent a shard of ice straight through his testes. Was he mistaken or did Patrice seem to be challenging him to intervene on the young woman's behalf?

When Dorian was certain that everyone had gone to their beds, he crept up the narrow stairwell that led to the attic room that had become their guest's temporary accommodations. At some point in the life of the house the space had been converted into a modest bedroom with a small *en suite* bathroom. It was the sort of room a cash-strapped family might rent out to a college student, but for the fact that its only window consisted of a round pane of glass that had been sealed permanently shut. It looked like a porthole in the cabin of a ship. There was also a latch on the outside of the door rather than on the inside, suggesting that the room was being used for more sinister purposes. Dorian had heard about the fate of the previous occupants. Could he change the fate of the current one?

She was asleep on the bed when he let himself in, her honey-colored hair fanned out against the pillow like the rays of the sun. It was warm in the airless room and she lay on top of the covers rather than beneath. She still wore the clothes she'd had on earlier, which had become soiled during her pursuit. Her arm dangled part of the way off the mattress, its wrist cinched by a long nylon cord connected to a metal ring that had been soldered into the wall. The tether allowed her enough freedom to move about the room and have access to the bathroom. If she tried to go any farther, the cord was knotted in such a way that it would cut off the circulation to her arm, resulting not only in pain but probably injury.

The exhaustion that shadowed her face didn't detract from her beauty. Like a flower growing out from a rancid cesspool, the purity that radiated from her seemed to defy the corruption in the house. Dorian could smell the perspiration on her body and tamped down the arousal that stirred at his loins, for beneath this smell was another, more pleasing female one whose contemplation would not serve him well. He had come here to protect, not defile. Seeing her was like looking upon an angel, had he believed in such things as heavenly beings—he knew only those from Hell. Then suddenly he knew her name.

Angel.

She stirred, but did not awaken. Instead she rolled onto her side, facing away from Dorian toward the porthole window. He had come to the attic in great consternation, expecting to find evidence of her having been tampered with by Patrice or one of the others. Indeed, even the women in the household were not incapable of molesting one of their own should the desire to do so arise. At one time he'd been amused and delighted by the clever application of their hands and various other implements to the bodies of their female victims as they coaxed out the final pleasure. The thought of them doing so to the young woman on the bed filled him with agony.

As Angel slept, blissfully unaware of the unimaginable horrors awaiting her when she woke, Dorian remembered when he too, had the capacity to sleep this way, like a child innocent of sin and corruption. The last time such a sleep had been his was before he'd sat for Basil Hallward. He had lived several lifetimes since then. Suddenly he felt the weight of all his years pulling on him—pulling him down into Hell. Had this young woman been sent here to offer him one last chance at redemption?

A long-dormant tenderness began to seep into Dorian's heart, warring with the wickedness that dwelled there. The hem of Angel's skirt had ridden up from her pose and his prick reacted at the sight of her buttocks in their scanty covering, inviting him to do his worst. His need to defile told him to take her in a manner which he suspected she would most rebel at, though why he was so convinced of her purity he had no idea. Perhaps it was because of how she'd appeared to him in The Dream—with all the ingenuousness of a young woman unblemished by the greed and cruelties of a corrupted lust.

The sunlight coming in through the porthole window turned the glass into a radiant eye, watching him, judging him, and once again Dorian experienced shame for his thoughts. Unlike the sweet shame he'd invited upon himself in a Marrakesh alleyway, this shame lingered on his palate like the taste of putrefying flesh. Moving to the other side of the bed, he lowered himself gently onto the mattress so as not to waken the sleeping woman, reaching out to smooth her hair back from her damp forehead. He brought his fingertips to his mouth and licked them dry. They tasted of honey.

He was losing his mind.

Rather than assembling in the parlor with their guest as planned, Patrice instead issued instructions that no one in the household was to disturb her other than to deliver meals and liquid refreshment. This task was assigned to Athenie, who'd never made a secret of her preference for men, even in matters of blood. For this at least Dorian was grateful, though he couldn't help wondering if Angel's supposed reprieve was some kind of trick to disguise from the others her real purpose in being here. Perhaps Patrice planned to take her for himself, draining her lifeblood while savoring the final tremors of her climax as she moved from life into death. This sudden cooling of his interest seemed artificial. Patrice had an agenda of his own, but what it was or when it would present itself was anyone's guess.

Though Dorian felt like a fool, he began to sleep outside the door to Angel's room like Cerberus guarding the underworld. He didn't trust himself to remain alone with her for more than a brief few minutes at a time, so from dawn until late afternoon he slept with his back against the latched door. His discomfort was minor compared to the alternatives. Yet neither Patrice nor anyone else in the household put in an appearance—not until early evening, when Athenie brought up a meal on a tray. Dorian assumed she would report his daily presence to Patrice and fully expected to be made sport of by both him and the group when they assembled for their regular activities, but nothing was ever mentioned. Rather than put him at ease, this put him further on his guard.

During the day while everyone slept and Dorian was on sentinel duty, Angel was awake, either moving about the room or performing her ablutions in the bathroom. She had taken to washing her few garments in the sink. Dorian would often discover her panties, bra, and blouse draped over the shower rail when he crept in at dawn to check on her. Occasionally these items were joined by her skirt, which still retained the smudges of dirt from her fall to the sidewalk. Whether Angel was aware of him at her bedside he knew not, though he'd noticed that she no longer slept on top of the bedcovers but beneath the sheet, the room being too warm for anything more. He knew from the garments drying in the bathroom when she was naked, and he continually fought the desire to pull the sheet from her body and commit the filthiest deeds he could conceive of committing. At times his need was such that he bit down on his fingers, not even realizing that his teeth had sawed through the flesh until the taste of his own blood flooded his mouth.

Then there were those moments when he thought that she'd heard him, though she never opened her eyes. He knew that she sensed his presence—just as she sensed it later as he reclined in a half-slumber against the door, guarding her with his life. "Please, will you let me out?" came a plaintive cry through the wood. Although the plea tore at his heart, Dorian was undecided what to do about her. If he tried to set her free, the likelihood was that she wouldn't reach the front gate alive. Only Patrice knew the code for the alarm, the presence of which Dorian suspected had less to do with keeping burglars out and more to do with keeping the residents of the house *in*.

Eventually she stopped asking.

When the second week of Angel's imprisonment went by with no incident, Dorian became convinced that Patrice was keeping her here as a test, using her as bait to see how long he could resist before committing the atrocities that haunted his sleep. Though his need was more for the corporeal than the sanguinary, he too wondered how long he could hold out. Never had he been in such turmoil—and there was no one to whom he could speak of it to ease his mind. There was no Lord Henry to tease and scoff and bring him to his senses as to what he truly desired. There was no Lord Henry to take away any misplaced sense of guilt should he act in a completely selfish manner. As for his companions, they were nothing but silly children—trying to discuss his inner turmoil with them was comparable to discussing a fine painting with a blind man. Although Patrice had come as near to dear Henry as anyone, Dorian distrusted him more than he distrusted himself.

Yet Dorian was not the only member of the household who'd become part of some twisted experiment. Despite their nocturnal forays into the city, there hadn't been a kill since before Angel's arrival. Whether it was by design or coincidence Dorian couldn't be certain, though he had his suspicions. It seemed as if Patrice wanted to starve their addiction, though he unreservedly approved the group's increasing use of illicit substances to appease their bloodlust. Even Dorian had begun to indulge more frequently, hoping the corresponding rush or calm would dull the sharp edges of his desire until he had figured out what to do about Angel. If she *were* to die in this house, he would rather it be at his hands.

One of the moments Dorian had been dreading finally arrived when Patrice summoned him into the parlor. "Far too much time has elapsed since we last indulged our passions," Patrice told him over a glass of port, apparently unconcerned that the others were listening. Dorian could see a smirk passing across Julien's face; Athenie was having difficulty keeping back a giggle. If the group hadn't been aware of their earlier intimacy, they certainly were now. Perhaps he shouldn't have been surprised. He had expected it to come sooner and, when it didn't, had wrongly concluded that the encounter had been a one-time event designed to show who between them held control over the other. When he made no reply, Patrice added: "Unless you think your little girlfriend might not approve?"

Dorian felt bile rising up into his throat. "I have no idea what you're talking about," he said, sounding unconvincing even to his own ears.

Patrice fixed him with a violet stare. "A man should not live his life by the dictates of women."

It sounded as if Lord Henry had spoken. Was Dorian to have no allies—not even the memory of a dead man? The thought of being with Patrice while his beautiful Angel waited for him on the floor above—waited for him to stroke her honey-colored hair as she timidly observed him beneath the fringe of her eyelashes—brought with it a pain worse than any he'd imagined. The little attic room was located directly above Patrice's bedroom. The likelihood of her overhearing every coarse grunt from their lips as their bodies crashed together in lust and loathing was such that Dorian could already feel the blight of shame eating away at his flesh.

"Perhaps we can invite her in to watch," said Patrice, reading Dorian's thoughts. "I am certain it will be quite an education for her. Would you enjoy that, my friend?"

At first Dorian refused. Patrice appeared to take it rather well, shrugging his shoulders as if it were of no consequence to him one way or the other. But all that would change when during that night's hunt their would-be victim—a lanky young man wearing a backward baseball cap—managed to escape into the bowels of a housing project. Dorian thought Patrice had been intentionally sloppy and allowed him to get away, thereby tormenting his followers with yet another victim they couldn't have.

By the time the man got away, the night had turned foul. The leaden sky opened up, sending lashes of rain down upon them, the wind whipping their wet hair into their eyes until they could barely see. A hurricane watch was in effect for the entire Gulf Coast, with dangerous thunderstorms predicted to hit New Orleans. Rather than continuing the chase, they returned home in frustration. The air crackled with need as they assembled in the front parlor, where they passed around a bottle of cognac, taking large gulps from it as if it were nothing stronger than flavored water. Hostility was thick in the air, most of it directed toward Patrice. They knew that pleasure awaited them in the attic—and no one could understand why he was depriving them of it.

For two days heavy thunderstorms continued to pelt the city, their winds and violent explosions of lightning adding further to the group's foul temper. They had been cooped up in the damp house since the night the young man they'd been pursuing had outwitted them. Their eyes remained fixed on the small television set Patrice had brought into the parlor as overly excited newscasters reported that the hurricane watch had been elevated to a hurricane warning. The story that had been running for the last two weeks about the young woman who'd gone missing after leaving work in the French Quarter had been pushed aside. Instead viewers were treated to end-of-the-world scenarios promising death and destruction. The possibility of floodwaters topping the levees and flooding the city had prompted local authorities to advise residents to evacuate or seek higher ground.

Although the Night People were unconcerned with such mundane matters as the weather, the chances of finding a new victim under these circumstances were severely limited. Having learned the harsh lessons of Hurricane Katrina, city residents were taking no chances. Businesses were being boarded up and the interstate was clogged with traffic as people sought to get as far away from New Orleans as their cars would take them. Those who couldn't leave were instructed to go to local shelters. The last flights had already left any airport within a hundred-mile radius. No one was getting in and no one was getting out.

Hoping the situation had been exaggerated, the group ventured out at dusk to see for themselves. Other than the occasional wind-whipped TV news crew, they were the only ones on the streets. The Quarter had become a ghost town. They returned home rain-soaked and defeated, though Patrice appeared curiously jubilant as he went upstairs to his bedroom to change out of his wet clothes.

Dorian could see that the five young people were at their breaking point. They didn't like staying in with the grown-ups; they wanted to go outside and play. Patrice remained for the most part oblivious, ignoring their grumbling and whining and fidgeting. He sat drinking his port as if it were just another evening in the parlor. He seemed to be intentionally going out of his way to irritate them with his indifference. Dorian could smell the tension in the room and it worried him. The camaraderie that had always been a mainstay for the group had vanished. The women were sniping at the men and at each other, and the men were doing likewise, even coming to blows over an offhand comment that was misinterpreted.

"It's not fair!" wailed Marceline.

"What's not fair, little one?" asked Patrice without interest. He stared out the rain-ravaged window, watching as the fountain in the walled garden overflowed with slimy green water.

"Why is she here if we can't have her?"

Dorian felt an anxious fluttering in his belly. Marceline was talking about his Angel. Other than the weather, she had been the sole topic of conversation from the moment they'd brought her home.

"Yes, why is she here if she's not for us to play with?" chimed Juliette. Suddenly her tone turned hopeful. "Is she for me? Is that why she's here—so I can have her first?"

Setting his glass of port onto the table, Patrice fixed Juliette with a toxic glare. "The young lady is to be left alone. If she is to be taken, *I* will be the one to take her. Is that understood?"

Although no one dared to speak or contradict his orders, the group glowered at him as if they could will him dead. Dorian also remained silent, but he was finding the uncertainty of Angel's fate intolerable. Was Patrice really saving the girl for himself? If so, what was he waiting for?

He received his answer later that night when Patrice summoned Dorian to his bedroom. "I expect you know why I've asked you to come to me." He moved toward Dorian, his boots making no sound on the old wooden floorboards whereas everyone else always sounded like a herd of angry cattle in their clumsy thick-soled boots.

"I confess that I do not," replied Dorian, remaining by the open door as if the escape it afforded could save him from what was to come.

Patrice reached out to caress Dorian's cheek, trailing his fingertips down the slope of his neck and over his shirtfront, not stopping until he had reached the flap of his trousers. He gave it a meaningful squeeze. "Oh, I think that you do." He leaned in close—so close that

Dorian was pressed up against the door, its glass knob lodging painfully between his buttocks as if it sought to violate him.

A loud crack of thunder shook the old house, causing the lamp by the bed to wink several times until it decided to stay on. "What is it that you want, Patrice? I'd like to retire early tonight." Indeed, Dorian *did* wish to retire early—and he planned to do so outside Angel's door. He had not liked the atmosphere in the parlor this evening. The desperation and dissent in the group made him question how much longer they would defer to Patrice's authority, particularly under the circumstances. They were behaving like animals trapped in a cage. It appeared that an act of nature might well be the Night People's ultimate undoing.

Patrice's tongue fluttered across Dorian's lips, leaving behind the tantalizing taste of violets. Dorian felt his prick jump in response and cursed inwardly. Despite everything that had gone on, he could not deny that Patrice was the most alluring man he'd ever seen. Only a few short weeks ago he would have given anything to worship Patrice's body, done anything he desired; now it was the last thing he wanted.

Unzipping the front of Dorian's trousers, Patrice slipped his hand inside the gap, grasping hold of his partial erection until it had attained full status. Dorian tried to convince himself that his response was strictly mechanical—no more exceptional than if he'd been touched by the hand of a cut-rate whore—but when he felt a betraying leak of moisture he hated himself more than he hated Patrice.

"I want you," said Patrice, tearing open Dorian's shirtfront to expose his smooth chest. The buttons clattered like hail onto the floorboards. He pushed the loosened waistband of Dorian's trousers down to his thighs, trapping him. "And I always get what I want."

When Patrice reached around to insert his finger inside Dorian, it felt as if a lightning bolt had entered him. "No!" he cried, trying to close his body to the digital assault.

"No?" mimicked Patrice, his scorn returning in full force. He gave the object in his hand a sharp pull, the pain shooting straight through Dorian's testes and into his belly, doubling him over. "Does *this* say 'no'?"

Dorian's positioning had made him more vulnerable for what came next as a second finger joined the first, his interior welcoming them in a clenching embrace that humiliated him as much as it pleased him. "Or does this?" hissed Patrice, manipulating his fingers skillfully to trigger a climax. It washed over his hand like a frothy wave hitting the shoreline.

Despite the evidence of his pleasure glistening in Patrice's palm, Dorian replied: "I no longer desire you."

Patrice began to laugh. It was a horrible sound—worse than the destructive winds that were shaking the house and rattling the windows, threatening to destroy the city. "What does desire have to do with it? I care nothing for what you desire. I merely want you to fuck me."

By now Dorian had regained his wits and could once again stand up straight, though he was still trapped between the door and Patrice's hand. "And if I refuse? What then?"

Patrice shrugged. "Then you refuse. It is entirely your decision, my friend. You are free to do as you wish. I do not hold you here against your will. But the young lady," he paused, his eyes looking meaningfully at the ceiling, "*she* is another matter entirely."

Dorian had known this was coming—that his Angel had been brought to this damp and crumbling old house full of bloodthirsty misfits to die. It was simply a matter of *when.*

Patrice resumed his stroking, his hand no longer cruel against Dorian's receptive flesh but instead sensual and seductive, as was his voice. "I shall take her," he said. "I shall drink every drop of blood from her body—and I intend to do so while I am fucking the life out of her." A skull's grin contorted his face. "And I will let you watch. If you are a very good boy, I may even let you taste her when she comes for the last time." An old and corrupt soul stared out through eyes that Dorian had once considered beautiful. "Do not even think of trying to spirit her away. Trust me when I say that neither of you will leave this house alive. I think you know me well enough not to doubt my power."

If Dorian had doubted before, he did so no longer. Patrice was a creature not of this world. "And if I do as you wish? Will you let her go free?" The thought of the atrocities Patrice so gleefully outlined devastated him. Yet perhaps what devastated him more was the knowledge that whatever transpired in Patrice's room would be overheard by her. By allowing Dorian to save her, Patrice intended to destroy the purity of her thoughts for the man who would act as her savior. To have his Angel see him through tarnished eyes seemed far worse than the prospect of her defilement and death. Dorian had known the price of her freedom would be high, but never had he imagined it would be *this* high. "And what of the others?" he ventured to ask. "How do I know they will keep to this bargain?"

Had Athenie noticed earlier this evening, when taking in the tray of food, that he'd loosened the cord at Angel's wrist—and if so, had she reported it to Patrice? Dorian could no longer bear to see the chafing and bruising on her delicate skin. He wanted to go to her right now and hold her in his arms. He wanted to tell her that what he needed to do was merely a means to protect her—if only he could be granted a moment to explain, so that she would not look upon him with disgust after it was finished. Suddenly Dorian couldn't remember if he'd re-latched the door when he had left. Maybe it would be better if she died while trying to escape rather than listening to the vile goings-on that would soon be taking place in the bedroom beneath her.

"I can assure you everyone is happily engaged elsewhere," Patrice replied with a sly smile. "I've given them a certain dragon to chase. We won't be seeing them till tomorrow."

For now, at least, his Angel was safe.

Stripping off his garments, Patrice let them drop right where he stood. It was a very different scenario from when he'd undressed with a studied leisure meant to infuriate Dorian. Now he appeared to be in a tremendous hurry as he fell backward onto the bed, his erection heavy against his belly. This time Dorian would be forced to look into Patrice's eyes when he took him. He felt himself being sucked into their violet depths as powerfully as he felt himself being sucked into the depths of Patrice's body, both of which refused to release their hold on him.

Draping his legs over Dorian's shoulders, Patrice raised his hips high to absorb each brutal thrust, his seed spraying his belly and chest each time he came.

He grunted like a rutting animal, shouting out Dorian's name again and again, knowing full well the sound carried up through the floorboards and into the attic room above. Even the explosive cracks of thunder could not drown out Patrice's voice as he broadcast his ecstasy to the household and, more significantly, into Angel's flushing ear.

The lamp on the bedside table flickered repeatedly as the storm took firmer hold, the terrible keening of the wind sending another shudder through the old house. It felt as though the walls were being squeezed in a vice—a sure indication that the hurricane was moving in. Dorian was also being squeezed in a vice as Patrice's interior clutched his immersed flesh with the arrival of yet another climax, intensifying Dorian's self-loathing as he felt his own climax squeezed out of him. "Yes, my dear boy, fill me with your pleasure!" cried Patrice. "Fill me till I burst!"

Dorian felt himself dying inside when he heard the sobbing coming from the room above. It made him want to tear open the man beneath him until his blood soaked through the mattress and into the floorboards. Yet the rage with which he took Patrice only gave rise to more satisfaction. A normal human being would never have survived such a fierce pummeling, but Patrice had reached a state of rapture. His face was radiant with an inner light, his violet eyes lifting heavenward as if he expected to be led into Paradise. Dorian was giving him exactly what he wanted. Could he trust Patrice to make good on the bargain and release Angel unharmed? Suddenly he realized that Patrice had not actually consented to her freedom. He had implied it, but he had never expressly said that he would grant it.

Dorian pulled out of the greedy void that seemed intent upon swallowing him whole. How could he have been such a fool? Patrice would *never* allow Angel to leave. He would do to her exactly what he said he'd do. That he would make Dorian bear witness to every nightmarish moment of it he had no doubt.

Patrice's eyes returned earthward, stabbing into Dorian like knives. "Our pleasure is not yet over, my friend."

"You have lied to me!"

"*Lied?* How so?"

"You never intended to let her go."

An evil smile contorted Patrice's features. "I assume you're referring to the young lady upstairs?"

Dorian had seen this smile before. He recognized it from his own portrait, before he'd locked it away beneath the earth. The creature before him was a monster—a thing far worse than anything Satan could have sent up from Hell. Dorian felt polluted; he wished more than anything that he could wash himself clean. He wanted to be as he was before his vanity had thrust him into the filth of his existence. "You know damned well to whom I'm referring," he snapped. The pungent aroma of the other man's ejaculate filled the room. Dorian smelled murder.

"Did I say I would let her go?" Patrice's insane laughter spiraled around the room like the eye of the hurricane that now spiraled around the city. "Why would I let her go when I have such delightful plans for her? Surely you, more than *anyone*, can appreciate this." Grabbing hold of his still-erect prick, he began to pleasure himself, his palm skimming rapidly over the crown. "You and I are the same," he said, his rapid breaths embracing Dorian with the scent of decaying violets. "I knew this from the instant we met."

"We are not the same!" shouted Dorian. "I am not like you!"

"But you are *exactly* like me, my friend. We have been crafted from the same rib." Patrice pushed his pelvis up into Dorian's face. "Now open your sweet mouth so that I may fill it with your special reward. You must be thirsty from your labors!"

At that moment the lamp flickered and went out, along with every light in the house. New Orleans had turned black, as did Dorian's fury.

Patrice began to come.

The sobbing overhead turned to terrified wails and Dorian felt his heart being torn from his chest. Love was an emotion he'd never expected to experience again. Although it had been soiled by lust, he knew that what he felt for Angel was true and good. He also knew that she wouldn't live to see the morning as long as Patrice remained alive.

Wrapping his hands around Patrice's neck, Dorian pressed his thumbs into his windpipe, calling on every particle of strength in his body to silence the sickening sound of the other man's pleasure as he felt it splashing hotly onto his chest. Suddenly the room was illuminated by a flash of lightning and he found himself staring down into Lord Henry's face. The flesh appeared blue, though whether this was from the effects of the lightning on Dorian's retinas or the termination of oxygen to the strangled man's lungs he couldn't be certain.

Fierce winds slammed into the exterior walls of the house, followed by the sound of breaking glass. Several downstairs windows imploded as the pressure that had been building up inside was finally released. As the eye of the hurricane moved directly overhead, an eerie rattle escaped from the crushed throat Dorian continued to hold in his hands.

And then it passed.

Dorian felt a blissful sense of peace as he lay down alongside the body of the man whose life he had just taken.

His Angel was safe.

EPILOGUE

BUCKINGHAMSHIRE COUNTRYSIDE, PRESENT DAY

Ned Piggott couldn't understand what had got into his cows today. They were making a frightful ruckus with their daft mooing and milling about. *A right lot of stupid heifers*, he mused, shaking his head in disgust. No wonder they ended up on the dinner table more often than not. As he stood looking out the kitchen window and drinking his heavily sugared tea, he saw them wobble, then collapse to the ground, as if they'd just spent too much time down the pub. He felt his blood go cold. He prayed it wasn't a return of BSE. "Mad cow" disease had decimated the livelihoods of farmers, not to mention its dire effects on the British economy. He'd be ruined if it infected his herd! It couldn't happen to him. He'd always been so careful, especially when it came to feed suppliers. He wasn't penny-wise and pound-foolish like so many others.

What Ned couldn't see, but the cows *could,* was that the earth had begun to bubble and churn in a volcanic mass of green and brown. The new spring grass looked as if invisible hands were ripping it apart until it had become nothing but clumps of semi-dry mud scattered in the field by the hands of a madman. Several feet beneath the surface of the ground, well out of view of Ned and his herd, lay a concrete bunker. It was from here that the source of the turmoil originated.

Inside the bunker, a painting covered over with a sheet sat on a wooden easel. Although age had turned the white fabric yellow, it couldn't take credit for the sickly yellow and rusty red that had spent the last century oozing forth from the painting's surface like bloodied pus, soaking into the sheet and drying in stiff, foul-smelling splotches. The painting had undergone considerable transformation since its inception, moving from a representation of youth, beauty, and innocence into something so gruesome that even to look upon it inspired terror. It had once been the portrait of a young man so exquisitely perfect in appearance that a woman or man would have instantly fallen in love with him.

And now it had become so again.

NEW ORLEANS,
PRESENT DAY

The hurricane's wrath had scourged the city, overflowing levees, flooding streets, and displacing most of those who had remained behind to ride it out. Property was destroyed; so were lives. Those who had survived the last such catastrophe did not survive this one. Those who did wished that they hadn't.

New Orleans had given birth to the lost people.

For weeks they could be found wandering the streets, trying to make sense of what had happened. Some were reunited with loved ones, while others were forced to identify the bodies of those whom they had loved. One of the lost was a young woman who grabbed the arm of anyone she encountered, launching into an incoherent babble about a house in the French Quarter in which she'd been held prisoner in the attic by a gang of Goth kids. One of the arms she eventually grabbed belonged to a New Orleans police officer.

When police finally had the time to investigate the young woman's bizarre claim, they discovered the bodies of three women and two men in the front parlor of the house she'd managed to identify. Without a proper forensic investigation, it wasn't possible to determine the cause of death—or even to guess at it. Other than broken glass from a window and water damage to the walls and floor, there seemed to be nothing that might explain how five outwardly healthy young people should suddenly die.

The situation was altogether different in an upstairs bedroom, where they found the nude body of a young man lying in bed. He had significant bruising at his neck, indicating that he'd probably met his death by some form of strangulation. The fact that his stomach and torso had a significant amount of what appeared to be dried semen on it pointed to his death likely being of a sexual nature. What police saw next led them to conclude that some form of voodoo had been involved.

For lying on the bed alongside the dead man was a small pile of men's clothes. They were covered with ash and fragments of bone that may or may not have been human.

ABOUT THE AUTHOR

Mitzi Szereto (mitziszereto.com) is an author and anthology editor of multi-genre fiction and nonfiction. She has her own blog, "Errant Ramblings: Mitzi Szereto's Weblog" (mitziszereto.com/blog) and a Web TV channel, Mitzi TV (mitziszereto.com/tv), which covers the "quirky" side of London. Her books include the epic fantasy-themed *Thrones of Desire: Erotic Tales of Swords, Mist and Fire*; the quirky crime/cozy mystery *Normal for Norfolk (The Thelonious T. Bear Chronicles)*; the Jane Austen sex parody *Pride and Prejudice: Hidden Lusts*; *Red Velvet and Absinthe: Paranormal Erotic Romance*; *In Sleeping Beauty's Bed: Erotic Fairy Tales*; *Getting Even: Revenge Stories*; *Wicked: Sexy Tales of Legendary Lovers*; *Dying For It: Tales of Sex and Death*; the *Erotic Travel Tales* anthologies; and many other titles. A popular social media personality and frequent interviewee, she has pioneered erotic writing workshops in the UK and mainland

Europe and lectured in creative writing at several British universities. Her anthology *Erotic Travel Tales 2* is the first anthology of erotica to feature a Fellow of the Royal Society of Literature. She divides her time between London, England, and various regions of the United States. Her next book, the Gothic-themed anthology *Darker Edge of Desire*, is forthcoming in fall 2014.

Red Hot Erotic Romance

Buy 4 books, Get 1 *FREE**

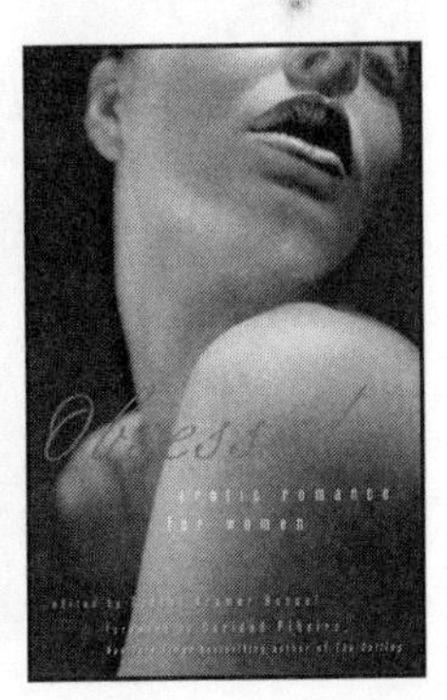

Obsessed
Erotic Romance for Women
Edited by Rachel Kramer Bussel

These stories sizzle with the kind of obsession that is fueled by our deepest desires, the ones that hold couples together, the ones that haunt us and don't let go. Whether just-blooming passions, rekindled sparks or reinvented relationships, these lovers put the object of their obsession first.
ISBN 978-1-57344-718-8 $14.95

Passion
Erotic Romance for Women
Edited by Rachel Kramer Bussel

Love and sex have always been intimately intertwined—and *Passion* shows just how delicious the possibilities are when they mingle in this sensual collection edited by award-winning author Rachel Kramer Bussel.
ISBN 978-1-57344-415-6 $14.95

Girls Who Bite
Lesbian Vampire Erotica
Edited by Delilah Devlin

Bestselling romance writer Delilah Devlin and her contributors add fresh girl-on-girl blood to the pantheon of the paranormal. The stories in *Girls Who Bite* are varied, unexpected, and soul-scorching.
ISBN 978-1-57344-715-7 $14.95

Irresistible
Erotic Romance for Couples
Edited by Rachel Kramer Bussel

This prolific editor has gathered the most popular fantasies and created a sizzling, no-holds-barred collection of explicit encounters in which couples turn their deepest desires into reality.
978-1-57344-762-1 $14.95

Heat Wave
Hot, Hot, Hot Erotica
Edited by Alison Tyler

What could be sexier or more seductive than bare, sun-warmed skin? Bestselling erotica author Alison Tyler gathers explicit stories of summer sex bursting with the sweet eroticism of swimsuits, sprinklers, and ripe strawberries.
ISBN 978-1-57344-710-2 $15.95

*** Free book of equal or lesser value. Shipping and applicable sales tax extra.**
Cleis Press • (800) 780-2279 • orders@cleispress.com
www.cleispress.com